WAKING
THE
WORLD

M.I.Five

Written by Matt Thomas
Designed by Tracey Cunnell
Edited by Pat Hegarty
Illustrated by Rob Davis

Cover background © iStockphoto

Created by WizzBook Ltd
Copyright © 2009 WizzBook Ltd
All rights reserved

First published in the UK
by Potter Books, RH17 5PA, UK

www.potterbooks.co.uk

Printed in the UK
by CPI Bookmarque,
Croydon, CRO 4TD

WAKING THE WORLD

THE

WORLD

Matt Thomas

Illustrated by Rob Davis

Potter BOOKS

WHAT HAPPENS NEXT? YOU DECIDE...

Five extraordinary kids are about to embark on an exciting mission to save the world. Armed with incredible talents, and determined to defeat one man's evil plan to achieve world domination, can the kids save the day? On four occasions you'll be prompted to choose from a selection of alternative chapters, and your choice will determine how the plot unfolds.

1
THE LETTER

It was an unusually quiet morning in East London. From Jake's bedroom, on the third floor of a large block of flats, you could normally hear sirens, cars and the general sounds of hundreds of people getting up and going to work. Today there was no noise, except for the serene sound of birds tweeting.

As the minute hand of Jake's alarm clock crept round to half past seven, the peace was shattered. A high-pitched ringing filled the room and Jake reluctantly opened his eyes. He hauled himself up, sat on the edge of the bed and rubbed his face until he felt awake.

He looked around his room. It was a mess. Maths books and puzzle books were all over the place, football kit was hanging over every chair, and his West Ham poster was coming unstuck from the wall. He was going to tidy up tonight, definitely.

It was the first day back at school after the summer holidays. Jake knew that most of his friends would be far from happy about returning to school after six weeks off, but he didn't mind. In fact, though he'd never admit it, Jake was happy to be going back. He missed the excitement of learning new things and couldn't wait to see his friends again – they hadn't been around much recently. Over the last week or so he'd struggled to find anyone to hang out with at all.

Jake pulled on a T-shirt and walked through the flat to the kitchen. His mum was a university professor and, like him, kept books all over the place. Jake yelped as he stubbed his toe on one of them. He picked it up – a gigantic hardback called 'Advanced Theories of Modern Mathematics' – and tucked it under his arm. He'd have a glance at that later.

In the kitchen, Jake's mum was frying sausages and flicking through one of her students' essays. She was a cheerful woman who was always smiling. She spoke quickly and waved her hands as she talked, as if she was excited about everything. Jake loved that about her – a lot of his friends' mums seemed pretty boring in comparison.

"Hiya, Jake," she said. "I've made up a new kind of sausage: parsnip and cod! Want some?"

"Okay, Mum," said Jake, wincing at the thought. Jake's mum was a very enthusiastic cook, though she could never manage a simple omelette or sandwich.

To her, cooking was an adventure and she always liked to try new things. Jake didn't mind too much. Sometimes the weird recipes worked – her apple pizza was one of his favourites.

She spooned two of the unusual sausages on to his plate and handed him a piece of toast.

"How are you getting on with *Lord of the Rings*?" she asked. Jake's mum loved books and was delighted that Jake enjoyed reading, too.

"I liked the ending," he said, with a mouth full of parsnip and cod.

"You've finished it already? You only got it two weeks ago!"

"I just got into it," replied Jake.

"It's a thousand pages long though, darling!" said Jake's mum, astonished at her son.

Jake shrugged his shoulders, a little embarrassed, and cut up his sausages. She patted him on the hand.

"You're a very special boy, Jake Robinson," she said, smiling. Jake focused even harder on his plate.

As he let himself out of the flat and wandered through the back streets to school, Jake thought about what his mum had said. He knew that she was only being nice, but it had made him feel weird, all the same. The thing was, he didn't want to be special. To him, special meant different. He wanted to be normal like his friends. They didn't read maths books for fun...they didn't always know the answers in class...why was he so strange?

Jake was so distracted that he almost didn't notice how quiet the neighbourhood was. At this time of day the pavements were normally filled with shrieking, yelling school kids and mums chatting, but today they were almost completely empty. Even more strangely, there wasn't a single car on the road.

Jake decided to pay a visit to the corner shop. Maybe sweets and some football stickers would cheer him up.

The electronic door chime bleeped as Jake walked in to find Mr Jackson, the owner, standing behind the counter, frowning at his empty store.

"Hi, Mr Jackson," said Jake.

"Oh, hello Jake," he replied, distracted. Jake chose his sweets and placed them on the counter.

"And a pack of football stickers, please," said Jake. Mr Jackson sighed as he turned to fetch the stickers. "See the match last night?" continued Jake, hoping to start a conversation. Mr Jackson frowned.

"No, Jake," he replied irritably. "I was working. I'm working all the time these days. Not that anybody comes in any more."

Jake could see that he was upset; he looked tired too. "Where's Paul?" he enquired. Paul was Mr Jackson's son and often took the late and early shifts to give his dad a break. Mr Jackson looked down at the counter and a shadow crossed his face.

"Paul no longer works here, Jake," said Mr Jackson. "He no longer does anything...just sits in his room playing that stupid computer game."

Jake hated seeing people upset, especially good blokes like Mr Jackson. He tried desperately to think of something to say to make him feel better, but couldn't come up with anything.

Mr Jackson took a deep breath and collected himself. "I'm sorry Jake, it's just very stressful, you know? Now, get to school before you're late." Mr Jackson tried to smile, but Jake knew the difference between a real smile and a fake: that one was a fake.

Jake felt sorry for Mr Jackson, but what had happened to Paul was not unusual. The game he was into was called Powerball. It was the only game available on a new console called the Razon 500 and everyone was talking about it. All of Jake's friends were playing it, even adults were into it – it was a huge craze.

Jake had never played it, though. His mum didn't approve of computer games: yet *another* thing that was different about his life.

As Jake walked along the road to school, the empty streets and pavements began to trouble him. Something was up. Jake didn't know what exactly, but it was strange, very strange indeed.

Jake stopped at his best friend Will's house. He thought there was time for a quick kick-about before school, to take his mind off everything. Will was his most football-mad friend, and you could always rely on him for a game.

He knocked on the door. There was no answer so he knocked again. Jake was about to give up when the door slowly swung open. Will was standing on the doorstep looking scruffy and exhausted, as if he'd been up for days.

"What do you want?" he said, irritably.

"Crikey, Will, what's up with you today?" said Jake, a bit put out by his friend's rudeness. "Just thought you might fancy a quick game before school?"

"I'm not going to school!" snapped Will.

"Why not?" asked Jake, shocked. It wasn't like Will to skip school.

"I'm playing Powerball. All the guys are," he explained with a roll of his eyes. "Now either come in or leave me to it!"

Jake paused. He was curious about the game of course, but missing school? Also, Will was being pretty mean. He decided not to go inside.

"No thanks, mate, I'm gonna go to school," Jake said, as he turned and walked away.

"Okay, weirdo!" shouted Will, as he slammed the door on him.

Jake sat in the form room on his own. None of the other kids had turned up yet. This morning was maths, Jake's favourite subject, but after what Will had said he wouldn't be able to concentrate. In fact, Jake felt like crying. Maybe he *was* just a weirdo? Everyone else hated maths lessons; everyone else was into Powerball. What was wrong with him? Why wasn't he more like his friends?

The door to the classroom swung open as Miss

Parry entered. "Right-oh class, settle down now, time fo..." Miss Parry trailed off as she realised that the class *was* settled down. There was only one pupil and he certainly didn't feel like making a noise.

She paused for a moment and then spoke.

"Jake...where on earth is everyone?"

"Dunno, Miss," said Jake, lying through his teeth. He knew exactly where all the other kids were: the same place they'd been for days, sat motionless in front of a Razon 500.

"Really?" enquired Miss Parry, not believing him for a second.

"Really, Miss," replied Jake, with no enthusiasm for the lie.

"Hmm. Well, their parents will all be receiving phone calls," she said, flopping into her chair at the front of the classroom, unsure of quite what to do with a class that had one pupil. "I don't think it's necessary to bother with the register, is it, Jake?"

"Probably not, Miss."

A thought struck Miss Parry and she smiled. "Actually, I'm glad I have you on your own right now. I have some rather exciting news."

"Miss?"

"It seems that word of your commendable performance in last year's exams has spread." She smiled and placed a letter on his desk. Jake picked it up, now completely confused.

> *Dear Miss Parry,*
>
> *After tracking the performance of star pupil Jake Robinson for several years we would like to offer him a scholarship (effective immediately) to the Sarah Moore School for Gifted Children.*
> *Our school offers gifted children of Jake's standard the space and stimulation to develop their intellect to the full. From what we have gathered, Jake's potential is practically unlimited. We're sure that with our help he will be able to achieve great things.*
>
> *Yours faithfully,*
> *Sarah Ellen Moore*
> *Headmistress, Sarah Moore School*

Jake put the letter down, looked up at Miss Parry's beaming face and frowned.

The rest of the day at school was very odd. As he was virtually the only kid there, he thought he'd get one-to-one attention in every lesson, but sometimes the teachers didn't even turn up. He ate lunch alone and when the bell went for hometime, he walked back through quiet roads and along deserted pavements.

Jake did not know what was going on around here, but he did know one thing for sure: he was not going to an exclusive school full of stuck-up, 'gifted' kids!

The place was probably full of toffs. He'd never be normal if he went there. He had to find a way of getting out of it, and fast.

As soon as he got home he tore the letter in half and threw it into the kitchen bin. Then he shut himself in his room and thought about the day he'd just had. He couldn't make sense of it. Where was everyone? They couldn't all be playing Powerball. What was so good about it anyway? And, even more worryingly, what the heck was the flipping Sarah Moore School for Gifted Children?

The questions were exhausting and he soon fell into an agitated sleep. When his mother called him for dinner he ate in silence and, after he had finished, went straight back to his room.

He read a maths textbook that he'd found that morning, hoping that it would take his mind off everything. At least numbers still made sense. He'd borrowed the book from the university library, but he'd pretended that it was for his mum. Jake had to admit that he liked the idea of going to university one day. His train of thought was interrupted by a knock at the door.

"Can I come in, love?" called his mum, through the door.

"Sure, Mum," replied Jake. She smiled awkwardly as she entered the room and sat down on the edge of his bed.

"You alright?" she said. "You seemed a bit down at dinner."

"I'm okay," said Jake, lying again. "Mum?" he continued, hesitantly.

"Yes, darling?"

"Can we get a Razon 500?" he asked hopefully.

A worried look came across his mother's face. "Jake. That Powerball game is for stupid people. Are you a stupid person?"

"Wish I was sometimes," mumbled Jake. His mother frowned.

"Jakey, there's something I need us to have a bit of a chat about."

Jake's heart sank as she produced the Sarah Moore letter. It was taped together and food-stained from the bin, but still very much readable. "I found it when I was throwing out the fish heads from the herring stew," she added.

Jake's heart sank as he looked at the letter. "I don't want to go, Mum," he pleaded.

"Why on earth not?" she replied, surprised.

"It'll be full of boffins," he said. "Please, Mum, I just want to be ordinary."

She thought for a moment, then looked at her son with compassion. "Darling, I know how hard it is being special, but believe me, you couldn't ever be ordinary." She tapped him on the head and smiled. "Inside there is a great gift."

"I didn't ask to be clever, Mum," croaked Jake, beginning to cry. He looked away, ashamed of himself and unable to meet his mum's eye. She gave him a hug and heaved a sigh, as if she understood what he was feeling.

"I know, darling, but you are," she said. "This Sarah woman is right. You're capable of extraordinary things and you have to go and do them. The Sarah Moore School sounds like a great place to start."

Jake thought carefully. Deep down, he knew that she was right. He wasn't really interested in computer games anyway, he was just a bit curious about this Powerball one.

"Promise me that you'll at least give the school a go?" she continued, smiling at him sympathetically.

Jake looked up at his mother and then back down at the maths book full of insanely complicated equations and exercises. If one of his friends picked up the book they wouldn't be able to make head nor tail of it, but he understood it. He understood it perfectly. That wasn't normal…he wasn't normal. Finally he took a deep breath and wiped away his tears. "Okay, Mum," he replied. "I'll try."

2
firST DaY

Jake's mum's old car shuddered and rattled as it struggled up the hill.

Jake stared out of the window. He didn't feel like talking. In fact, he still wished he wasn't going at all. The whole thing had happened too quickly; it was still only a week since Jake had been given the letter. After a long phone call with the school's headmistress, Jake's mum had excitedly taken Jake out of his old school and now, the following Monday, was driving him to deepest Cumbria to begin his new education.

"We're making great time, aren't we?" said Jake's mum, in an attempt to lighten the mood in the car. Jake didn't reply, although she was right; they'd got out of London in practically no time at all and had barely seen another car, even on the motorway!

That was strange. Actually, it was more than strange, it was sinister. Nobody seemed to be doing anything any more: the shops were empty, all football matches had been stopped temporarily, hardly anybody was turning up to their jobs. It was as if the whole country had decided to stay home. Nobody could explain it, but, then again, nobody was trying to. The whole nation was simply letting itself slide.

A large manor house began to appear from behind the crest of the hill. Jake had never seen a house so big. That couldn't be the school – surely!

"Here we are," said Jake's mum a few moments later, as she swung the car through the school's grand but rusty gates.

As the car bounced down the badly kept drive, Jake's eyes widened with astonishment. The school was huge! However, as they got closer, they began to see more detail. Whilst it was still very grand, it had clearly fallen into disrepair: moss and algae were growing on every surface, some of the walls were crumbling, and the windows badly needed cleaning.

The only new thing about it was a sign painted above the door that read 'Sarah Moore School' in bold, bright letters. If Jake didn't know better he'd have said that the paint was still wet.

Jake's mum brought the car to a standstill outside the front door and smiled at her son, although it was clear that she was on the verge of tears. "Now, you're sure you packed everything?" she asked.

"Yes, Mum," Jake replied.

Jake's mum kept thinking of questions until finally, when she ran out of things to worry about, she simply said, "Good luck, darling."

"You mean you're not coming in?" asked Jake, suddenly concerned.

"I'd love to," she said, "but it's against school policy. The headmistress insists that all children get their first impressions of the place 'without parental interference'," said Jake's mum. "It all sounds very progressive," she added, grinning broadly.

Jake didn't want to dent his mother's enthusiasm so he smiled back, though he certainly did not share this Sarah woman's eagerness that he be left alone outside a strange school in the middle of nowhere. Jake got out of the car, as his mum handed him two suitcases out of the boot. She hugged him and smiled, tears forming again in her eyes.

"You're going to have such a great time," she said. "I'm quite jealous." Jake grabbed her and hugged her as tightly as he could.

"There's a peach and tuna sandwich in your bag if you get hungry, and I'll call you tonight." She ruffled his hair and got back into the car. Then, with a wave, she was gone.

As Jake watched the car drive into the distance, a thought struck him. This was the first time that he had ever been away from home. He felt a mixture of fear and, to his surprise, excitement as he turned and climbed the steps to the front door.

He pushed hard and the giant slab of oak creaked against its ancient hinges. The room on the other side was not what Jake had expected. There was no reception desk, no signs to direct visitors and, most strangely of all, no noise. In his experience schools were noisy places, filled with activity. This room didn't look like anything had happened in it for a long time.

He looked around; there were no signs of life. For a moment he wondered whether he was in the right place. He couldn't remember anything else outside but grass and hills around for miles.

He stood alone, taking in the giant reception room. It didn't look like any school he'd ever been in. A huge, rickety staircase on the opposite side gave access to the upper floors and dominated his view. There were stern looking portraits and antiques lining the walls, and everything was covered in a thick layer of dust.

There was no sign of another human being in the whole place. Jake was alone.

There was only one thing for it. "Hellooooo?" he shouted up the stairs, the sound of his voice echoing around the building.

No reply. This was peculiar. There had to be someone here, it was a school. He filled his lungs for another attempt, but stopped when he saw some movement at the top of the giant staircase. A girl, Jake guessed about twelve years old like him, was waving at him.

"Hello," she replied, gracefully descending the staircase. As she got closer Jake could see that she was pretty...very pretty.

"Jake, I presume?" she said, offering her hand.

"That's right," he managed to reply as he shook her hand. Jake expected her to tell him her name at this point but instead she simply smiled.

"Come on, there are people you need to meet," she said.

With that, she began walking quickly up the stairs. Jake grabbed his suitcase and hurried after her.

Jake had expected to be greeted by Sarah Moore herself, or at least by a teacher. To have a fellow pupil showing him around seemed really odd. But maybe that was just the way they did it in genius schools.

The girl led Jake to a small room filled with computers. Wires, hard drives and disks covered the floor, and a huge bank of monitors took up an entire wall. In one corner, a small girl was tapping away at a keyboard. Jake didn't notice her immediately; she seemed so at home with the technology that she almost blended in. She was a small, tomboyish girl, probably about ten years old, with long, shiny black hair scraped back into a ponytail.

"Chun Mai!" said Jake's guide loudly. The girl jolted suddenly, surprised to see them. She was so engrossed in her task that she hadn't even noticed them entering the room.

"Oh, hi," she replied.

"This is Chun Mai," said the girl. "She's our computer specialist. In fact, Chun Mai is one of the best computer programmers in the world."

That can't be right, thought Jake. Admittedly, he didn't know much about programming but he knew that it was incredibly complicated stuff that required years of experience. How could this girl have risen to such a high level at her age?

"Stop, you'll embarrass me," said Chun Mai with a grin. She didn't look embarrassed at all.

"This is Jake," said the girl.

"Pleased to meet you," said Chun Mai, offering her hand. Jake went to shake it but, as soon as their palms touched, an electric shock passed through his arm. He pulled his hand away in surprise. Chun Mai giggled as she showed him the electric shock buzzer concealed in her palm.

"She may be a genius, but unfortunately she has a five-year-old's sense of humour," said the girl.

"I'm sorry, Jake," said Chun Mai. "Here, have one of these – my way of apologising." She offered him a tube of crisps which Jake gratefully accepted but, as he opened the lid, springing snakes popped out. Jake leapt backwards, tumbling over a chair.

Chun Mai laughed so hard that she fell off her own chair. Wiping tears from her eyes, she stood and offered her hand to pull Jake to his feet.

"It's okay, I'm fine," Jake mumbled. He might not be a genius programmer, but he wasn't stupid enough to fall for the same trick twice.

"Come on, let's go," said the girl, who was smiling quietly to herself. "There are more people to meet." They turned and left Chun Mai to her private hilarity.

Confusion was not a feeling that Jake was too familiar with and it definitely wasn't one he enjoyed. With every moment that passed he was becoming more and more agitated. He didn't even know this girl's name, for goodness sake!

She led him to another door. "I didn't catch your name," said Jake to the girl as she knocked.

"That's because I didn't throw it," she replied. That was all Jake needed – someone else with a rubbish sense of humour. Being a genius and a comedian didn't seem to go well together.

"Robert, are you in there?" the girl said through the door. There was no response.

They were about to turn and go when a loud "Enter!" came from the other side of the door. Jake and the girl did as they were told, but when they got inside there was no one around.

"Robert, where are you?" said the girl. "I thought you were in here?"

Suddenly there was a flash of light at the other end of the room and Robert appeared out of a puff of smoke. He was a tall, blonde boy dressed in designer jeans and a shirt. He was standing with his arms raised aloft, as if expecting applause. Unfortunately the girl didn't look like she was going to give him any.

He dropped his arms, slightly deflated, and looked at the girl. "I'd appreciate it if you called me Roberto, not Robert," he said grumpily, in one of the most upper-class accents Jake had ever heard.

The girl sighed. "'The Great Roberto' is your stage name, Robert. I don't see a stage."

"All the world's a stage!" Robert replied theatrically, as he flounced across the room to pour himself a glass of water. Jake wasn't used to hearing people speak like this, except for the Royal Family on the news.

"Robert's a magician," said the girl, rolling her eyes and waving her hand in his direction.

"Young Magician of the Year, three years running, *actually*," he said, smirking as he sipped his water.

"Whatever, Robert," the girl said as if she'd heard this fact many, many times before.

"Who's this?" asked Robert, addressing the girl rather than Jake: something that Jake's mother had always told him was very rude.

"This, Robert, is Jake," she replied. "He's going to join us."

"Is he now?" replied Robert snootily, looking Jake up and down.

Jake was really starting to dislike this boy but he thought he'd at least attempt to make friends. "That was a great trick," he said. "How did you do it?"

Robert looked at Jake haughtily. "As if I'd tell you."

Jake's anger grew. Why was he being so rude? Jake hadn't done anything to him.

"Come on, Jake," said the girl, sensing that there was about to be an argument. "We'll come back when he's in a better mood," she added, steering Jake out of the room and shooting Robert a pointed look as they left.

Back in the hallway, they walked down a different corridor. No doubt they were going to see another crazy 'genius' – Jake was completely baffled and still very angry.

"Where are all the classrooms?" he asked bluntly, as the girl led him back down the giant staircase. Receiving no answer, he pressed on with another question. "Why haven't I met any teachers yet?" Again, he was met with silence.

"Can you at least tell me your flipping name?!" he exclaimed, stopping in the middle of the hallway to demand a response.

"Don't worry about details yet," said the girl finally, as if a few words from her officially closed the subject. "There's one more person I want you to meet."

She led him out of the school to a huge, overgrown field at the back. In the distance they could see a boy almost covered by the thick grass. He was wearing a lab coat and standing next to a large metal pole.

"Alex is an inventor," said the girl. "He's brilliant. The things he's created over the last few weeks will blow your mind!"

Jake's mind was already well and truly blown. Inventors? Magicians? Computer programmers? This had to be the weirdest school in the world.

"Alex!" the girl shouted across the grounds as the boy pressed a button on the top of the pole.

When Alex noticed them he began to wave frantically and ran towards them. As he got closer they could just about make out his words. "Get back, get back!" he yelled. "Magnet, magnet!"

Jake only had time to wonder if all genius inventor kids repeated everything twice, before he found himself flying through the air.

A high pitched ringing filled his ears and he saw the girl, arm outstretched like a superhero, flying alongside him. Alex ducked for cover as Jake and the girl struck the pole with a heavy thud.

Alex came running over and hurriedly pushed the 'Off' button on the pole, allowing Jake and the girl to slump to the ground.

"I'm *really* sorry. I didn't think anyone would be out here when I was testing – it picked up the metal in your watches!" gasped Alex, rapidly. "Are you okay?"

"What on earth is that thing?" asked the girl as she rubbed her wrist angrily.

"Basically, it's just a really powerful magnet," said Alex. "I thought it might be good for disarming people, y'know, if we're attacked."

"Who's going to attack a school?" asked Jake as he stood up and dusted himself down. He was thoroughly fed up with all this nonsense. He needed somebody to explain things to him right now.

"Umm..." said Alex looking at the girl apologetically, as if he'd let something slip.

Jake picked up on this immediately. After being talked down to, lied to and hurled through the air, he was in no mood for any more messing about.

"If somebody doesn't tell me what's going on right now, I'm walking out!" said Jake. "This isn't a school at all, is it?"

"Jake, look – " said the girl.

"No! I've had enough!" Jake interrupted, "I want answers. First of all, what *is* your name?"

"Okay," the girl sighed, seeming irritated at the situation being forced out of her control. "My name is Sarah Moore."

Jake's mind reeled. Sarah Moore? That was the name of the school's head teacher. But how was that possible?

"You're the woman who's been talking to my mum on the phone?" asked Jake.

"I do an extremely good adult voice," said Sarah, perfectly impersonating someone five times her real age. "You're quite right, Jake," she continued, "this isn't a school."

3

WHAT'S going on?

Jake was used to knowing more than most people around him, and being this mixed up was putting him on edge. He didn't like secrets and this whole place seemed like one big lie.

He was sitting alone at the end of a mahogany dining table, roughly the size of his bedroom, his mind racing as he tried to decide whether he felt angry, confused, or a mixture of emotions he didn't even have the words for. Sarah had asked him to wait in the huge hall while she collected the rest of the crazies that populated this so-called 'school' in order to explain themselves.

Finally, the door creaked open. Sarah and the others walked in and sat opposite him.

"I'm sorry we had to lie to you, Jake," said Sarah. "But it was the only way to get you here without risking a security breach."

"Security breach?" said Jake. "What're you talking about? Just tell me what's going on!"

Sarah looked at the other kids and paused for a very long time before responding.

"Have you noticed anything strange happening recently?" asked Sarah eventually, clearly choosing her words carefully.

"You mean besides being sent to a fake school?" replied Jake, sarcastically.

"For goodness sake," interrupted Robert. "She's talking about the game."

"What game?" asked Jake.

"The game everyone's been playing constantly for the last few weeks!" Robert replied.

"You mean Powerball?" asked Jake.

"Yes, of course I mean Powerball!" said Robert, exasperated.

This guy is pushing his luck, thought Jake. He would have stood up for himself, but right now he was simply too confused. "What's Powerball got to do with anything?" he asked. "It's just a craze!"

"I wish that were true, Jake," said Sarah. "Chun Mai, perhaps you should explain this part."

"Alright," said Chun Mai. "Prepare yourself though, Jake, this is a lot to take in," she warned as she took a deep breath.

"My older brother loves computer games," she began. "A few months ago he got into Powerball, before anyone else had really heard of it, and over the next few weeks he changed completely. He wouldn't eat properly, he wouldn't talk to anyone, he barely even slept. He just played Powerball. Before long, my parents were playing it too," Chun Mai said. "They still are," she added solemnly.

Chun Mai's face had changed. The cheeky grin that Jake had seen earlier had been replaced by a look of deep sadness. Everyone else had begun to shift uncomfortably in their chairs. Jake remembered Will and the blank, bleary-eyed look on his face the last time they'd met.

"I was suspicious," Chun Mai continued. "This really wasn't like them. So I looked into Razon, the company that make the game."

"By 'looked into' she of course means she hacked into their computer system without the company realising," said Alex with obvious pride.

"Well, naturally," said Chun Mai, a teeny bit of her former chirpiness creeping into her voice.

"And?" asked Jake, fascinated.

"You have to understand, I've hacked into a lot of computer systems," said Chun Mai, with all the world-weariness of someone much, much older. "Government, military – you name it, I've broken in," she continued, bragging a little now. "But Razon has the most secure network I've *ever* come across."

"Which is strange in itself," said Alex. "You wouldn't

think a computer games company needed to be quite so careful, would you?"

"Unless, of course, they have something to hide," added Sarah.

"Precisely," continued Chun Mai. "And here's another thing. Most computer games makers have offices in busy cities like London or New York. Razon's main office is an old sewage works in the middle of the Polish countryside."

"That sounds like a pretty weird place to have an office," said Jake.

"Again, not if you're trying to hide something," said Robert, irritably.

"Anyway, it took a solid week, but I managed to get into the network," she said, proudly.

"And what did you find?" asked Jake.

"Prepare to be blown away," said Robert under his breath. Jake heard, but wasn't sure if he was taking the mickey. He chose to ignore it.

"Razon are using Powerball as a stage one neuro-programming device," said Chun Mai.

Jake looked back at her blankly.

"Their Powerball game is hypnotising people," explained Sarah.

Jake took a moment to take in what was being said to him. According to Chun Mai, a computer games maker had put a large section of the world's population into a hypnotic trance. It sounded preposterous, but it did make some sort of crazy sense. The huge change in Will, Paul and everyone else exposed to the game was too shocking to be pure coincidence.

Jake realised that the four were all looking at him. They were clearly waiting for a response, but Jake didn't have one. He could only wonder out loud, "Why?"

Sarah frowned, "That's what we don't know."

"But you can bet your life this isn't the end of it," added Alex.

"That's right," agreed Robert. "Jake, can I assume that you don't know anything at all about hypnosis?" he said, smugly.

"No, I don't," said Jake, through gritted teeth.

"Well, I do," continued Robert. "I use it in my illusions all the time." He stood up and began to pace, milking his moment in the limelight.

"It's like a deep sleep," he said, "except your eyes are open and you can understand things said to you, although you won't remember them when you wake up." Robert paused for dramatic effect. "The trouble is, you're in a vulnerable state. You don't have your normal common sense, so you can be made to do absolutely anything by the person who hypnotised you, even if it's harmful to you or to someone else."

"But the people aren't doing anything," said Jake. "They're just sitting and playing."

"You mean they're not doing anything *yet,*" said Robert. "Believe me, there's more to this. Razon haven't hypnotised half the world for a laugh."

"Half the world!?" said Jake, truly shocked.

"We think that Razon currently has about three billion people in a state of full hypnosis," said Alex.

"That's around half the population of the world," said Sarah, solemnly.

"And the rest aren't far behind," said Robert, grimly. "In a few days Razon will probably be able to make two thirds of the world's population cluck like chickens if they want to."

"Though somehow I doubt that's what they're planning," added Sarah.

Five minutes later, the meeting had broken up and Jake was outside.It was all too much; he had to take a minute to think, away from the others, and the rambling, overgrown garden seemed as good a place as any. He found a seat on the edge of a large fountain that, like everything in this manor house, was decaying fast.

With his head spinning, Jake tried to take in what he'd just heard. Could it really be true? It seemed improbable that a sinister company could enslave half the world without more people noticing, and impossible that the only people capable of exposing them would be four freaky kids.

"I know how you're feeling," said a voice from behind him. It was Sarah. Jake had been so deep in thought that she had been able to walk right up without him noticing, even through the thick grass. "When they told me, I freaked out too," she said.

"I'm not freaking out!" he snapped. "It's just..." Jake trailed off. He *was* freaking out, he was very much freaking out – but something about Sarah made him want to impress her. He wanted to look as if he was taking it all in his stride, when really he felt as if his head was about to explode.

"Whose manor house is this, anway?" Jake asked, wanting to talk about something else for a moment.

"It belongs to Robert's family, but no one's lived here for years," explained Sarah. "It's safe."

"You guys should tell someone about all this, you know," Jake said.

"We're telling you," she replied.

"No, I mean – "

"Who, Jake?" asked Sarah. "A journalist? The government? You think Chun Mai didn't try? Adults have closed minds to things like this. They've been around for so long, seeing things done in a certain way, that they can't believe something unexpected like this can happen, especially when the information is coming from a child."

She was right. Jake thought about what the adults he knew would say if he told them. Not even his mum would have believed him.

"The only people who'd believe in something like this are kids, Jake," said Sarah. "That's why they chose a computer game, their plan was to get us first." She continued, "It almost worked, too. By the time Chun Mai figured out what was going on, most of us were already playing the game. She found me, Alex and Robert just in time."

Sarah paced up and down. "If we don't stop this, the world is going to be a very different place," she sighed. "And it won't be a change for the better."

"Suppose I believe you," said Jake. "What has it got to do with me?"

"I want you to help us stop them," said Sarah.

"What?" blurted Jake as he laughed out loud at the sheer ridiculousness of it all. This was the sort of thing you saw in comic books or movies. Could it really be happening to him?

Jake stopped laughing as Will's pale, drained face flashed into his mind. It made him aware of the seriousness of the situation. This wasn't a comic book, this wasn't a movie; it was real. Someone had robbed three billion people of their freedom. Those people hadn't done anything to deserve that. He thought about the kids and grown-ups across the world sitting in their homes, trapped by the game; the people imprisoned by their TVs; the people who'd had their lives put on hold for no reason at all.

Sarah looked Jake straight in the eye and continued. "So I guess that only leaves one question," she said. "Are you in?"

Jake exhaled deeply. "I'm in," he replied.

4
Brady One

Jake and Sarah wandered back through the grounds. Neither spoke; Jake was still turning over the whole thing in his mind and Sarah could see that he wasn't in the mood for a chat. That morning Jake had been just another kid; now he was supposed to save the world? He couldn't get his head around it.

Jake's thoughts were interrupted as he noticed the other three kids in the distance.

"What's going on there?" he asked.

"I'm not sure," replied Sarah.

The kids were standing around a large white object with what looked like a rubbish bin strapped to the side. As they approached the group, the white object began to look more and more like a space rocket. Jake shook his head at the thought – his mind must be playing tricks on him.

"Oh," said Sarah, "that must be Brady One!"

"Oh, right, thanks, Sarah," said Jake, "that explains everything."

Sarah smiled. If she detected Jake's sarcasm she was choosing not to respond to it.

As they approached the group Alex beamed at them. "Ah, just in time," he said. "Allow me to introduce you to Brady One! Named after the great inventor: yours truly, Alex Brady."

"It looks like a space rocket!" exclaimed Jake, astonished and more than a little impressed by the strange object standing before him.

"That might be because it is one," replied Robert, rolling his eyes.

"Actually, Robert," explained Alex, "the space rocket is only the mode of transport, Brady One is this little baby."

Alex tapped the metal cylinder attached to the rocket. Close up it looked less like a rubbish bin, though it still had a homemade feel about it. It appeared to have solar panels and a telescopic camera lens at the front. What are they up to now? wondered Jake.

Alex noticed Jake's confused expression. "It's a satellite," he explained.

"We're going to use it to spy on the Razon Corporation HQ in Poland," said Chun Mai. "We can take photos, see what's going on, maybe even identify who's coming in and out, depending on the quality of the images," Chun Mai had noticeably brightened up; she was clearly looking forward to playing with this new toy.

"Hopefully, it'll help us figure out what Razon are actually up to," added Sarah.

"That's amazing!" said Jake. Just when he'd thought this day couldn't get any stranger, it had. He couldn't believe that someone his own age had managed to build a satellite and a space rocket all by himself. Well, assuming it worked, of course.

"Oh, nonsense. Satellites get launched all the time – there are over eight thousand orbiting Earth right now," Alex said matter-of-factly. "It's not rocket science! Well, I mean, it *is* rocket science obviously, but still, it's not *that* complicated."

"Sure," said Jake feeling a little intimidated by this boy's intelligence.

"Is it big enough?" said Sarah, looking at the four metre tall rocket. "I mean, it's got to go quite high, hasn't it?"

"Should be okay," said Alex. "We're only putting it into low orbit."

"So, about two hundred miles up?" said Jake, glad that he had a little knowledge about the subject.

Alex looked over at him, impressed. "You know about rockets?"

"Not really about rockets," said Jake, "but I've read a bit about planets, general astronomy, you know…"

"Well, you do seem like the sort to 'take up space'," said Robert, laughing at his own mean joke.

To Jake's relief, nobody else laughed and Robert looked at the ground, embarrassed.

Alex handed Jake a notebook. "Well, if you're into that sort of thing then have a look at this," he said. "All my calculations. Flight angles, weight…you've got to do a lot of maths to make sure a rocket flies right."

Jake took the notebook gladly and began flicking through the pages, eagerly taking in the numbers. There were very few people who could have understood what Alex meant by all the scribbled figures and symbols but Jake was pleased to be one of them. He ran his finger down the rows and his brain made sense of the numbers almost automatically.

He could actually imagine the course of the rocket.

"Come on, Alex," said Chun Mai. "Is it launch-time? We're hungry for success!"

The rest of the kids laughed and joined in the excitement, encouraging Alex to get on with it.

"Okay," he said finally, "I think we're ready!"

The kids moved a safe distance away, chattering excitedly – it was everyone's first space mission.

"Good luck Brady One!" he said, as he pressed the 'Enter' key on his laptop. The word 'Ignition' appeared on the screen, alongside a countdown timer. The kids began to count along, "Ten, nine, eight..." All except Jake, who was still looking at Alex's calculations.

Jake didn't know that much about space flight but he did know about maths and physics. He couldn't put his finger on it, but *something* was wrong with Robert's calculations. "Seven, six, five..."

Suddenly it hit him. "Stop!" he shouted, as the countdown continued... "Four, three, two..."

Jake desperately pushed past the others to get to the computer. He quickly clicked a button marked 'Countdown Pause'.

They all stared at him, shocked. "What do you think you're doing?" said Robert.

Jake ignored Robert and turned to Alex. "Alex, I think you've made a mistake in your calculations."

"Where?" asked Alex.

"I don't think you've allowed enough for the

45

weight of Brady One on the side of the rocket. I think it's going to pull it off course." Jake pointed at a section of the notebook. "See?"

Alex looked at the notebook, thinking carefully.

"Don't listen to him, Alex," said Robert. "You know what you're doing!"

"Hang on, Robert," replied Alex. "I'd better just check these calculations one more time."

"Nonsense!" said Robert haughtily, hammering the 'Enter' key.

"No!" yelled Jake, as a massive 'One' filled the computer screen.

There was a loud rumbling as the engines of the rocket fired. Suddenly a white-hot flame burst from the base of the rocket, causing a huge plume of smoke to erupt. The rocket began to lift off the ground, slowly at first, but soon picking up speed and rising up high into the clouds.

"See," said Robert, "no problem!"

Unfortunately for Brady One, Robert had spoken too soon. The moment that he finished speaking, the rocket began to bend off course: only slightly at first, but then more and more until it was obvious that the rocket was curving round into a wide arc.

"Oh, no!" said Alex.

Slowly, but surely, the rocket turned full circle and was soon pointing back towards the ground, returning to its launch pad like a boomerang. Alex's eyes widened with fear as he realised that the nose of the rocket was pointing straight at them. The rocket hurtled towards them, looming larger by the second.

"Umm, guys," said Alex, "now might be a good time to start running."

The kids scattered in all directions as the rocket bore down on them – and not a moment too soon as, with a huge crash, the rocket hit the ground and a tremendous ball of fire erupted.

The kids were knocked off their feet by the force of the blast and curled themselves up into balls, protecting their heads as a shower of earth rained down around them.

As the crash of the explosion faded from his eardrums, Alex carefully picked himself up. He looked at the massive crater and the still flaming remains of Brady One and sighed. He walked towards the crater and stared mournfully at his beloved invention.

Jake wandered over to Alex, who was still a little dazed from the blast. "Sorry, mate," he said, patting him on the shoulder.

"You were right!" Alex replied, frowning. "I guess I'll need your help with Brady Two."

The rest of the kids joined them and stood gazing at the wreckage, trying not to think about how close they'd come to being blown to smithereens.

"Anybody got a plan B?" asked Sarah, as she brushed dirt out of her hair.

5

Hoverpods

Jake picked his watch off the cabinet in the dusty, ramshackle bedroom and looked at the time. Eight o'clock: he'd get up now. Jake had been awake for hours. In fact, he wasn't completely sure that he'd slept at all. The revelations and near death experience of yesterday had left him with too many thoughts whirring around his head to be able to sleep. He just lay awake replaying everything in his mind until he felt as if he was going crazy. Maybe he was.

He felt both mentally and physically drained as he dragged himself out of bed and fished in his suitcase for something to wear. His mum had packed a load of smart, stuffy clothes – apparently thinking that genius children always dressed like they were going to a wedding. Luckily, when she wasn't looking, Jake had hidden his beloved West Ham shirt and a pair of jeans at the bottom of the case and these were what he pulled on. After all, if he was going to help save the world, surely he could wear what he wanted?

When Jake reached the kitchen he immediately regretted his decision. Robert, Chun Mai and Sarah were sitting around the kitchen table eating croissants and reading newspapers while classical music played softly in the background. Jake looked and felt completely out of place.

So, now I know what child geniuses do for breakfast, he thought.

"Hi, Jake," said Sarah when she saw him loitering at the door. "Want something to eat?"

"Do you have any cereal?" he asked.

"Sure, shredded wheat or muesli?" replied Sarah.

Suddenly Jake wasn't quite so hungry. He'd been thinking more along the lines of something involving chocolate, or at least some sugar. "I'll just have some toast," he murmured.

On his way to the breadboard, Jake edged past Robert and noticed that he was reading a maths textbook. He glanced at the pages full of equations and numbers and couldn't help taking a closer look.

"Can I help you?" said Robert testily, as he noticed Jake peering over his shoulder.

"Are those sequence problems?" asked Jake, ignoring the rude tone in Robert's voice.

"Yes, they are, if you must know," said Robert.

"Mind if I have a look?"

"Be my guest. But I warn you, they're pretty tough. I've been stuck on this one since last night," said Robert, pointing to a particular problem.

"This should be a laugh," said Robert under his breath as Jake took the book.

Sequence puzzles are all about finding the next number in a series. Jake loved them. To him they were like mini detective stories. He looked carefully at the sequence of numbers that Robert was having trouble with, letting his brain take them in.

4, 8, 32, 512, ___

A couple of seconds later he grabbed Robert's pen and wrote 131,072 in the space. Flabbergasted, Robert flicked to the back of the book where the answers were: it was right!

"Did you just do that problem in your head?" asked Sarah, impressed.

Jake smiled. "You just multiply the first number by itself then divide it by two," he said. "Four times four is sixteen, divided by two is eight; then you do the same for the next number. Quite simple, really." Jake handed the book back to Robert and went to make his toast.

"I make that, Jake: one, Robert: nil," said Chun Mai under her breath.

"Told you," said Sarah to the still amazed Robert.

"He couldn't have figured that out from just looking at it," said Robert. "That's impossible! He obviously cheated somehow."

"Oh, Robert, get over yourself," said Sarah. "Remember the rocket yesterday? He figured that out in seconds...he's one of us."

"He's a genius!" added Chun Mai.

"No, I'm not!" protested Jake. "I'm normal! I just like numbers, that's all!" Angrily, he unwrapped a piece of gum and stuck it in his mouth, chewing down hard.

The kids were surprised by Jake's outburst. Who wouldn't want to be called a genius? They looked at him in stunned silence. Sarah opened her mouth to say something but before she could find the words, Alex had appeared at the door.

"I've done it!" he shouted. "They're finally ready!"

His hair was a mess, his face was covered in soot and there were holes burnt in his lab coat, but he was grinning like a crazy person. His excitement captured the whole group who, it seemed, knew what he was on about. They jumped up, and followed him as he dashed back into the hallway, giggling madly.

"Come on, Jake!" said Sarah, as she hurried out. Jake did as he was told, although he had absolutely no idea what was happening. In this place, though, that was nothing new.

"What's going on?" he asked Sarah. "Another rocket already?"

"No," she replied, "something better."

The kids sprinted out of the manor house, through the grounds and into a large barn at the end of the garden. They chattered excitedly as Alex stood panting in front of two bulky, round objects covered by a large dark sheet. He took a moment to catch his breath, before speaking.

"After months and months of painstaking work that nearly drove me insane," he began, "I, Alex Brady, genius inventor, have finally broken through one of the last frontiers of modern – "

"Give it a rest, Alex," interrupted Chun Mai. "We wanna see the hoverpods!"

"What's a hoverpod?" asked Jake.

Alex smiled. "Only one way to answer that question!" He pulled the sheet away to reveal two metal contraptions the size of very small cars.

They had what looked like mini jet engines bolted to their sides and no wheels. If Jake was brutally honest, they looked a bit strange and clunky.

"The age of traditional air travel is over!" stated Alex proudly. "Ladies and gentlemen, I present to you – the hoverpod!" Quiet descended upon the barn as the kids took in what they were seeing.

Eventually, Jake broke the silence. "Air travel?" he said. "You're telling me those things can fly?"

Alex looked a little insulted by Jake's lack of faith. "Not only do they fly," he pronounced, "they're capable of speeds of up to three hundred miles per hour."

"That's the speed of a passenger plane!" said Jake, impressed, as he walked up to the strange machines to get a closer look. Jake had always loved the idea of flying; he was one of the few people around that still looked up whenever he heard a plane overhead. The whole idea of air travel fascinated him; he had read several books about aeroplanes, though he'd never actually been in one.

"That's not all," said Alex, as he approached the cockpit of one of the hoverpods. He leaned in, pressed a button and the hoverpod disappeared. The kids gasped collectively. Even Robert, who was used to seeing things like this, was taken aback. However, as they stared at the space where the hoverpod had been and their eyes began to adjust, they saw what had happened.

The hoverpod hadn't disappeared – it had simply changed colour to exactly the same shade of grey as the walls of the barn, hiding itself almost perfectly.

"I wanted to make them invisible," said Alex, "but unfortunately that is scientifically impossible." He shook his head as if he was disappointed with himself. "However, fingers crossed, this camouflage function should make it pretty safe to fly around anywhere without being detected."

Jake pressed his hand against the dark grey shape. "It's amazing," he said, "absolutely amazing! I'd love to see it fly."

"How about you go one better?" said Alex, with a glint in his eye. "I need a test pilot."

Jake hesitated. Could he really fly one of these things? Was it safe? What if he crashed it?

Robert piped up. "I'll do it," he said, "if the maths whizz is too scared…"

"I'm not scared, Robert," growled Jake, angrily.

"Excellent!" said Alex. "Two hoverpods, two pilots. You can both fly."

"What do you say?" said Robert to Jake, smirking.

Jake had had enough of Robert's cockiness. And he certainly wasn't about to let Robert, or anyone else, call him a chicken.

"You're on," replied Jake.

6
THE race

Having agreed to become one of the first two people in the world to fly an experimental aircraft, designed and built by a boy who appeared to be just a little bit mad, Jake was feeling slightly nervous. Alex himself had not helped matters much with his pre-flight pep talk, which consisted mainly of instructions on what to do in the 'highly unlikely' event of an engine failure, a steering failure or any of the other million things that could go wrong with an untested flying machine.

If anything like that did happen, Jake was to bail out, pull his parachute cord and pray for a soft landing. He looked at the bolted-together contraption that he was going to fly – a failure with it seemed pretty likely! Jake looked across the grounds to the large crater that Alex's last invention had made when it had exploded, and wiped some nervous sweat from his brow. Robert swaggered up to his hoverpod and clambered in, looking nowhere near as tense as Jake felt.

"See you up in the sky, partner," said Robert sarcastically, as he slammed the hoverpod door shut behind him.

Petrified though Jake was, there was no way that he was going to let Robert win. He climbed into his hoverpod and looked at the handwritten piece of paper that Alex had given him as 'instructions' on how to fly it. Alex assured him that the hoverpod was very simple to operate. Jake wondered if Alex would be quite as confident if he was the one about to test it out.

He stuck the instructions to the dashboard with his piece of gum and pressed what was apparently the ignition button. He felt the machine rise effortlessly into the air. For a moment he was giddy with the thrill of flying the thing. It felt like all his best birthday mornings rolled into one.

Alex's voice crackled through the hoverpod's radio. "Right, guys," said Alex. "Keep climbing until you hit a hundred and fifty metres, then we'll begin the test."

Jake looked out of the window and watched the manor house shrink below him as he soared into the clouds. As he saw the digital display register '150m' he eased off and let the machine come to a stop, hovering like an enormous bird of prey. He looked out of the window and saw Robert's hoverpod alongside, hanging effortlessly in mid-air. It was an extremely peculiar sensation.

"Right, guys," said Alex over the intercom. "Have a look on your digital screens – you should see a map."

"Roger," said Robert.

"Umm, me too. I mean, Roger too – sorry, just Roger, Alex!" said Jake, flustered by the aviation language. He frowned as he saw Robert sniggering to himself in the other hoverpod.

"Now, on the map there are three checkpoints," said Alex. Jake looked down at the digital map and saw three blinking red dots. "I want you to fly to all those destinations then back here for debriefing. Got it?" Alex continued.

"Roger," said both boys simultaneously.

"Great, good luck!" said Alex.

"Hey, Jake," said Robert over the radio.

"What?" said Jake.

"Race you back to base!" he replied.

Before Jake had a chance to respond, Robert had fired his engines and his hoverpod was already speeding off into the distance.

"Oh no, you don't," said Jake. With a quick look at the 'instructions', he fired his own engines and raced off in pursuit. The kick of the acceleration pinned Jake to the back of his seat and, as he saw the clouds zipping past, he couldn't help but let a huge grin spread across his face.

The first checkpoint was ten miles away, but they were bearing down on it fast. Noticing that he was very slowly closing in on Robert, he kicked the boosters into overdrive to try to catch him at the turn. When they hit the checkpoint, Jake stamped on the airbrakes so that he could round the corner sharply. This thought hadn't occurred to Robert who sailed into a wide arcing turn, allowing Jake to pull alongside.

On the ground, Alex and Sarah were using the

laptop to follow the progress of the two hoverpods. Neither was particularly happy that the test had suddenly turned into a macho display.

"Boys!" huffed Sarah, frustrated. "Why does everything have to be a competition?"

Alex didn't hear her; he was too worried about his hoverpods getting wrecked.

"Guys, take it easy!" he shouted into the radio.

High above them, neither of the boys were in the mood to listen. They rounded the second checkpoint neck and neck, only centimetres apart.

"Guys!" Alex tried again. "At least listen to this: you're about to fly over a town. Go into camouflage mode now or you might be spotted."

Jake looked out of his window and saw Robert's hoverpod all but disappear. He pressed the camouflage button and his own machine disappeared from view.

Suddenly he felt a tremendous jolt from the side. "Sorry, old boy," came Robert's voice over the radio, "didn't see you there."

Yeah, right, thought Jake as he focused on the third checkpoint. Robert could play dirty if he wanted to, but there was no way he was going to win this race.

"Slow down!" yelled Sarah over the intercom, followed by a very panicky Alex.

"Don't smash up the hoverpods! Please don't smash up the hoverpods!" he cried breathlessly.

As they blazed through the final checkpoint, both boys came out of camouflage mode and Jake could see that they were still locked together. It was going to come down to the final race back to the manor house. Jake gritted his teeth and pushed his boosters up to the maximum.

WHAT HAPPENS NEXT?
YOU DECIDE...

Crash...
turn to page 64

No smoke without fire
turn to page 68

CrasH...

Robert was only a couple of metres ahead and the gap was decreasing rapidly. Jake moved to Robert's right to overtake but, at the last moment, Robert swung his hoverpod into Jake's path.

Jake had two choices. He could either have a mid-air collision, or he could take evasive action. Quickly, he jammed the joystick hard right and slammed on the brakes. He avoided Robert, but soon he had a new problem: he was out of control. The hoverpod began spinning wildly. Jake tugged at the joystick, frantically trying to get the thing back on course, but he couldn't. It was hopeless.

Adrenaline pulsed through Jake's veins as he saw the manor house rushing up to meet him. He was on a straight collision course with the east wing. Jake was gritting his teeth for the impact when the joystick suddenly began to respond. He managed to briefly regain control, pitching the hoverpod to the right. He knocked an engine clean off against the side of the manor house but narrowly avoided a full on crash.

With only one engine left, the hoverpod went into an uncontrollable barrel roll. There was nothing Jake could do but brace himself for impact with the ground. He closed his eyes tight and held his breath. The hoverpod hit the earth hard, bouncing and rolling along the grass, pieces flying off in all directions.

Before Jake's hoverpod had even come to a stop, Sarah and Alex were rushing over to the crash site. Sarah leapt on to the wreckage and began picking through the debris to get to the cockpit. She breathed a huge sigh of relief when she saw Jake looking up at her, apparently uninjured.

"Are you alright?" she asked, offering him her hand. He took it and hauled himself out of the wreckage.

"I think so," Jake replied, as the two of them climbed off the stricken hoverpod.

Alex was staring at the shattered flying machine, growing angrier by the second. "Do you know how long that took to build?" he demanded.

"Come on, Alex," said Sarah. "It was an accident."

"Don't get angry with me," replied Jake. "I could have been killed in that crash!"

"Well, that was your own fault," said Alex, coldly. "Hoverpods are not toys, Jake!"

"I know," said Jake. "It wasn't my idea to race."

"But you could have said no!" retorted Alex.

Alex was right. Jake had let his competitive pig-headedness get in the way of the job he was supposed to be doing. He was as much to blame for the crash as Robert was. Jake felt about five centimetres tall as he looked at poor Alex standing forlornly in front of his mangled invention.

"I'm sorry, Alex," he said, but Alex couldn't hear him; he was too busy picking through the wreckage to see what, if anything, could be salvaged.

The other hoverpod touched down gently next to them and Robert stepped out.

"You alright, Jake?" he asked.

"Yeah – no thanks to you," replied Jake.

"Hey, it's not my fault you couldn't handle the pace," said Robert. "Maybe you should stick to the puzzles, maths boy."

"For goodness sake, Robert," said Sarah. "Learn when to shut up!"

The conversation quickly deteriorated into a full-blown argument. Amidst all the noise, it was a miracle that Sarah heard her phone ring. It was Chun Mai, who had gone back to the computer room instead of watching the race. Sarah could tell that Chun Mai was very agitated, though she couldn't hear a word she was saying over the din of the argument.

"Everybody be quiet!" she screamed at the top of her voice. The boys stopped immediately, shocked at the outburst.

"Could you repeat that, Chun Mai?" said Sarah, returning to her natural, calm tone of voice.

"You guys need to get back over here right now," came the swift response from Chun Mai. "Something terrible is happening!"

Now continue to page 72

no smoke
without fire

Jake's hoverpod began to shake and shudder as it pushed top speed. This worried Jake a little, but he was catching Robert – he couldn't slow down now. Jake finally shot past Robert just before they reached the manor house. He blazed past the building's elaborate chimneystacks, whooping in victory.

Jake set the hoverpod down near Alex and Sarah and unbuckled himself. He hopped out of the machine triumphantly and saw Alex running over, presumably to congratulate him.

"Mate, that was amazing!" said Jake. "These hoverpods are..."

Jake tailed off as he saw that Alex was carrying a fire extinguisher. He ran straight past him to the hoverpod. Grey smoke was coming from one of the engines. Alex sheltered his face as flames flickered upwards, then doused the engine with the extinguisher before turning to Jake angrily.

"How fast were you going?" asked Alex.

"I don't know exactly," said Jake.

"I do," replied Alex. "You must have been pushing top speed the whole trip. This engine's completely fried!"

"I'm sorry, Alex," Jake replied. "But you didn't tell me there was a speed limit!"

"I didn't expect you to be daft enough to get involved in a race!" said Alex.

Jake's heart sank. Alex was right, it had been irresponsible. He was just about to apologise when Robert, who had landed in the middle of the drama without anyone noticing, walked towards them, clapping his hands slowly.

"Nice work, Jake," said Robert. "*Niiice* work."

"Hang on a minute, Robert, you were flying just as fast," said Sarah.

"No, Sarah, I think you'll find I was flying better," he said. "This idiot should never have been up there!"

This was too much for Jake and he finally lost it. "What exactly is your problem with me?" he shouted, his face close enough for Robert to smell the minty gum still on his breath.

"This is an elite group – and I don't think you have what it takes!" responded Robert. "Having someone around who isn't up to scratch is dangerous. You could get us all killed!"

Sarah's mobile phone rang.

"Hey! I never asked to come here," replied Jake.

"Then why don't you leave?" said Robert, bitterly.

"Everybody shut up!" yelled Sarah, holding her phone to her ear. The boys were so taken aback by Sarah's outburst that they did as they were told.

Sarah listened with growing anxiety. "Okay," she said into the phone before hanging up.

"It's Chun Mai," she continued. "We have to go to the computer room right now, something's happening... Only if the three of you have finished your hissy fits, of course."

Sarah had had enough of all of them. She turned on her heel and marched back to the manor house. The boys called a temporary truce and followed her, each one sensing that when they got there the news would not be good.

7
THiNgS geT worse

TV had suffered since the Powerball craze took hold; in the absence of staff at the TV stations, most channels were nothing more than a static logo. The only programme that was still on regularly was the news, although the chance of seeing a story that wasn't related to Powerball, and how great it was, was slim.

When the kids got to the computer room, they found Chun Mai nervously biting her nails as she watched a news bulletin.

"It's much worse than we thought," said Chun Mai, gesturing to the screen.

"What's going on?" asked Sarah.

"The Prime Minister just made an announcement." She shook her head in disbelief. "They're replaying it now, see for yourself."

The kids turned their attention to the screen.

Jonathan Holmes, the Prime Minister, was standing behind a row of microphones next to a large man with a jagged scar over his left eye. The Prime Minister looked tired and irritable, his tie was loose around his neck and his hair was a mess; he reminded Jake of Will.

"Thank you all for coming at such short notice," said the Prime Minister to the small gaggle of journalists who had bothered to turn up. "The man to my right is the inventor of the Razon 500 and Powerball, the greatest computer game ever made."

There was an enthusiastic round of applause from the TV as the kids looked at each other in disbelief. The Prime Minister continued, "Powerball has enhanced the lives of all who have played it, making us happier and more intelligent as a country. That is why, with effect from today, every household in the country will be required by law to own a Razon 500 games machine and a copy of Powerball."

The kids gasped in horror; could it really be true? Had they even got to the Prime Minister?

"And now, without further ado, Alain Razon," said the Prime Minister, introducing the man on his right. He moved to the side of the stage, applauding as he did so. The man gave a smarmy smile and took his place behind the lectern.

"Good evening, Britain," he said in a heavy French accent. A shiver ran down Chun Mai's spine; she was sure she'd seen that man before somewhere. "I thank your Prime Minister, Jonathan Holmes, for that kind introduction. My company is happy to supply everyone in the country with a Razon 500 free of charge."

"I bet it is," said Robert.

"Your very own Razon 500 will be with you by

the end of the day. However, be warned..." the man added, his face growing stern. "Anyone who refuses our gift will be breaking the law and will receive a heavy punishment." He let the message sink in before returning to his evil grin. "Though I'm sure that will not be necessary. Britain and the Razon Corporation have a great future together, you can count on that."

With that, he left the stage. Robert clicked off the TV and the kids sat in horrified silence, processing what they had just heard. By the end of tomorrow the whole country would probably be under the Razon Corporation's spell and there was nothing that they could do about it. Finally Sarah broke the silence.

"I knew that something like this would happen eventually," she said, "but I really thought we had more time."

"At least things can't get any worse," said Alex.

"Umm, I'm afraid that's not quite true," said Chun Mai, tapping frantically at her computer keyboard. "I knew I recognised that man on the TV, and I think I've just remembered where from."

"Well...?" said Robert.

"His real name's Jean-Paul Laurent," said Chun Mai, gravely. "I saw him on MI6's most-wanted list a few years ago. He's a French criminal who specialises in illegal arms dealing. He travels to war zones and sells weapons to both sides – making sure that the wars last long enough for him to make a good profit," she added. "He basically makes money out of other people's death and misery."

She tapped the 'Enter' key. "Here's his MI6 file." A giant picture of Jean-Paul flashed up on the screen, next to a short biography. A collective shudder ran through the kids as they stared at his cold grey eyes.

"Should you have access to MI6 files, Chun Mai?" said Alex.

"I think that's a conversation for another time, don't you?" replied Sarah.

"Hang on, Chun Mai," said Robert. "This file says 'deceased' at the top – that means he's dead."

"No, it means they *think* he's dead. He was caught up in an explosion two years ago while trying to steal an experimental weapon from the British Army. Unfortunately, it appears that he survived," said Chun Mai. "I'll give you three guesses what he was trying to steal," she continued.

Sarah sighed, "I'm guessing it was something to do with mind control."

"That's right," said Chun Mai. "The British Army have been working on a hypnotic computer programme for years. John-Paul must have copied it and faked his own death to cover his tracks."

"Then turned the programme into a computer game," added Robert. "Brilliant!" The kids looked at him in disbelief. "What?" he said, innocently. "You've got to admit, it is pretty clever."

76

"What do you think he wants?" asked Alex.

"I don't know," said Chun Mai. "But one thing's for sure, he's the last person in the world that I'd want to have this much power."

"So we have to stop him," said Sarah, standing up. Sarah was a very practical person; she saw no point in moping around. Even though she was terrified of this man and what he could do to the world, the news had only made her more determined to defeat him. "We need a plan," she said. "Jake, you've been very quiet, any thoughts?"

Sarah didn't get an answer. Jake wasn't there to give one. Amongst all the commotion no one had noticed him slip away.

8
no going BaCK!

By the time the kids had noticed his disappearance, Jake was already well on his way. He travelled cross-country to the nearest town; he didn't want to risk being found on the roads if they tried to follow him. He walked through cow fields and climbed over fences for what seemed like hours until, with mud caked on to his shoes and trousers, he finally found his way to a train station.

Then there was nothing to do but wait, and wait, and wait some more. The station, like the town he'd just walked through, was deserted. He sat like a statue for three hours, occasionally looking up and down the lonely train track and frowning. After the second hour he had given up all hope of a train actually arriving. Now the only thing keeping him there was the fact that he really had no idea what else to do.

Going back wasn't an option. He'd made his

decision and he didn't regret it; he didn't belong there. He wasn't a hero like those kids: the morning's hoverpod race had proved that. As much as he hated to admit it, Robert was right – if he tried to fool himself into thinking he should carry on, there was no telling what damage he might cause.

The main reason he was leaving, however, was his mum. Up until now, with no Razon 500 in the flat, she had been safe, but now Jean-Paul's men were giving out consoles like sweets it was only a matter of time until she was exposed to Powerball. He glanced down the tracks again frantically. He needed a train to come, badly! Every second he wasted, he imagined the Razon Corporation closing in on his flat. He needed to get there…he needed to stop them!

Then Jake had his first piece of good luck all day. He heard a noise in the distance, and when he looked down the track he could see an old, rusty-looking train emerging over the horizon. Jake smiled; he was finally going home.

The train came to a squeaking, shuddering stop and the driver leaned out of the window. He was a kindly looking old man, clearly nearing retirement, just like his train. "Hello?" he said, as if he was surprised to see him. "Going to London?" he asked.

"Yes, please," said Jake.

"Hop aboard then," he replied. "You're a lucky boy. I'm the only one going there today, apparently," he said, puzzled. "Can't think where everyone's got to."

"They're playing Powerball," said Jake, gloomily.

"What's that then?" said the man smiling. "One of those computer games, is it? Don't know anything about all that me'self, I don't even have a telly," he added, chuckling.

Jake decided not to tell him about Powerball; he'd find out for himself soon enough. Far better that he should enjoy his last few hours of blissful ignorance. Jake envied the man deeply as he climbed aboard the carriage, immersed in his own thoughts.

Several hours later, the train pulled into Euston station.

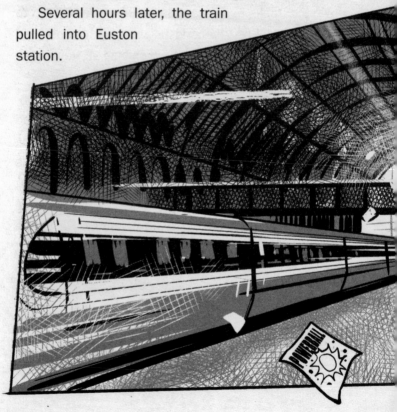

"Cheerio!" called the driver as Jake walked off, down the platform. Jake managed a thin smile before heading into the main station.

What he saw took his breath away. Usually it was crammed, day and night, with people rushing to their trains as they travelled around the country – but now, nothing.

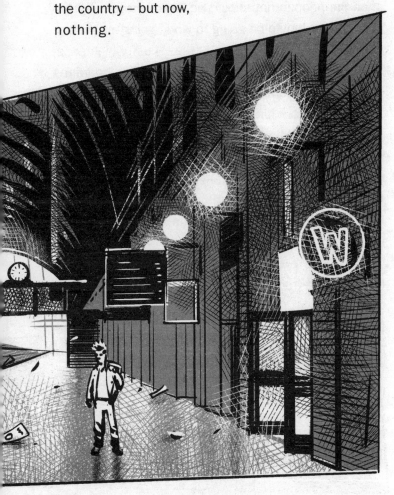

The place was completely empty, the shops and stands were abandoned, the only movement in the place came from the adverts playing on the TV screens and the rubbish blown around by the wind.

Jake had never felt more alone in his life. How had things got this bad? He felt like crying as he thought of all the people that should be here right now, all the people that should be going to work, going on holiday, seeing friends.

Suddenly the blank, joyless face of Jean-Paul filled every giant screen in the station.

"Greetings, citizens!" The words reverberated around the building. "The Razon Corporation thanks you for your support. Soon we will be one global family – and from there, anything is possible!" The face smiled and then faded to black, replaced by the Razon logo with the ominous tagline: 'Razon: Preparing the World for Tomorrow'.

Jake was overcome with rage. He couldn't stop this madman from taking over the world, but maybe he could stop him from turning his mum into one of his followers. He just had to get home in time! He had to get her somewhere safe.

He sprinted out of the station. He assumed that the underground would be out of action and he couldn't see any buses, or taxis. He looked left, then right, and saw nothing but deserted streets. It was as if a giant hand had picked up London and shaken all the people out. To see one of the busiest cities in the world looking like this was very creepy indeed.

Jake began to run. His flat was miles away, but he would have to get there under his own steam. He didn't slow down for an hour. Sweat and tears streamed down his face as his muscles and lungs burned – his whole body screamed at him to stop, but he wouldn't.

"Please Mum, hang on!" he said out loud to himself as he pelted past the tall buildings of the city and the surrounding tower blocks and estates. He saw the menacing glow of TV screens playing Powerball through every window as he went. He couldn't believe that it had come to this. Finally, he found himself on his own street. He came to a stop outside his block of flats, panting and struggling to catch his breath.

WHAT HAPPENS NEXT? YOU DECIDE...

**Jake finds
his mum**

turn to page 86

Will finds Jake

turn to page 91

jake finDs His mum

Jake took a deep breath and opened the front door to his block of flats. He climbed the stairs, dreading what he might find. His heart sank as he approached the door and found it ajar. Jake walked in; the place was completely dark apart from a flickering blue light coming from the living room. As he drew closer, a bad feeling grew in his stomach.

He walked into the living room, to be met by the most heartbreaking thing he had ever seen – his own mother with a control pad in her hands, staring blankly at the TV screen.

"Mum!" he shouted.

After a moment she turned and looked at him. "Hello, Jake," she said. "Come and play."

Jake looked at his mother: her blank expression, her bleary eyes. He began to cry. She was just another of Jean-Paul's pawns now. Soon Jake's mum's eyes were drawn away from her crying son and back to the TV screen. Jake looked too; he couldn't help it, the swirling blue-grey colours of Powerball felt comforting somehow. He smiled and began to relax. Was Powerball really all that bad? Surely one game couldn't hurt? Why not try it?

"No!" Jake said out loud. "I can't!"

He made a lunge across the living room and yanked the Razon 500's lead out of the wall.

"Nooooo!" came the scream from Jake's mother, as she bounded across the room. She drew back her hand and struck Jake across the face, leaving him sprawling on the floor as she scrabbled to put the plug back into the socket.

Jake looked at his mum, desperately clawing at the cable. She wasn't the same woman any more. She forced the plug into the wall and Jake watched her face in horror as it relaxed back into its pale, vacant state and she resumed playing.

Jake realised that he was completely alone in the world: no mum, no friends, just him. He felt a painful knot of sadness tighten in his stomach. Suddenly the game was interrupted as the TV flickered and the face of Jean-Paul filled the screen.

Jake glared at the screen as Jean-Paul began to speak. "We are approaching the moment of truth," he said. "The great plan is nearing completion. Soon I will give you your final instructions."

What was going on? What was 'the great plan'?
Jake wanted to find out more but as he watched Jean-
Paul speaking, he again found himself
being sucked in, his resistance
fading by the second.

In this situation most people would have simply stopped trying; they would have let themselves fall into the easy slavery of the game. After all, it was comfortable: there was no sadness in Powerball world, no pain, no loneliness. Most people would have just given up by now.

But then, Jake wasn't like most people.

He forced himself to stand up. He knew that he had to go. All the sadness that Jake felt had been replaced by a blinding, white-hot rage towards Jean-Paul. He gave his mother one last long look before bolting out of the flat. He didn't know where he was going or what he was going to do; all he knew was that he had to get out of there.

He ran out on to the street and stood, confused, for a moment. What was he going to do? Jean-Paul was communicating directly with players of the game, and now his own mother was one of them.

Just then, he heard the sound of a car's engine at full speed. Normally that wouldn't be a big deal in East London, but today?

Jake looked down the road and saw a bright red sports car approaching quickly. The car screeched to a halt in front of him. To Jake's surprise, it was Sarah behind the wheel! "Hey Jake!" she said. "I assumed this was where you'd be. Need a lift?"

Jake opened the door and climbed into the front seat. Sarah crunched the gears as she pulled away.

"Whose car is this?" asked Jake.

"You know, I'm not sure," replied Sarah. "I found it in the garage."

"Should you be driving?"

"It's not like there's much to crash into, is there?"

Jake looked around the empty London streets. Sarah had a point.

"They got to your mum, didn't they?" continued Sarah, carefully. Jake nodded, sadly. "I thought so. Chun Mai reckons they'll have control over everyone in the northern hemisphere by the end of the week," she added, grimly.

Jake took a ragged breath as he looked out at the empty streets. Sarah continued. "You need to help us, Jake. It's the only way left to – "

"You don't have to convince me," he interrupted, with a quiet determination in his voice. "Jean-Paul is going to pay!"

Sarah smiled. She slid the car into sixth gear and accelerated, back to Cumbria.

Now continue to page 97

WiLL fiNDS jake

Jake looked up at his window in the block of flats. He saw the blue flicker of a TV lighting up the window and sighed. He was about to run in when a noise from the other end of the street made him jolt with surprise. He hadn't heard anything except his own feet on the pavement since his arrival in London, but suddenly the air was filled with the sound of footsteps and voices.

He looked down the street and saw a mob of people rounding the corner. Something told Jake that he didn't want to be spotted, so he dived behind some bins. As the group came closer Jake could see that it was huge, probably more than three hundred people. What were they all doing? he wondered, though for now he could live without finding out. He huddled behind the bin praying that he wouldn't be spotted as he heard the mob storming past.

Jake's heart sank as he heard a voice from the crowd. "Hey, you!" it said. "What're you doing behind there?" Jake looked up and saw a dark figure looking down at him. "Jake?" it said.

Jake recognised that voice. "Hey, Will," replied Jake, trying to sound as calm as possible. "What's going on?"

"The Master's making an announcement and we're going to watch it at the park," said Will, blankly. "You will come with us."

The Master? thought Jake. He must mean Jean-Paul. Jake was curious about what this announcement was about but, even so, it sounded like a party he didn't want to attend.

"No thanks, I'm going to watch the announcement at home," said Jake, continuing with the ridiculous charade that everything was normal. "You know, with my mum."

Will had been joined by three other boys that Jake recognised from school. "You will come with us," they said in unison.

There was only one thing for it; Jake was going to have to run. He turned to escape but one of the other boys was too quick and tripped him up. Jake clattered to the ground painfully. He wasn't allowed to stay there for long, though, as the boys soon picked him up and held him aloft as they rejoined the group.

Jake struggled but he couldn't free himself from

their grip. It wasn't long before they reached Victoria Park, where a giant sheet had been stretched out to form a massive screen. A projector was shining Powerball's demo mode on to it. A crowd of thousands stood staring up in awe.

Suddenly the light flickered and a familiar face appeared on the screen. It was Jean-Paul. The crowd murmured respectfully.

"We are approaching the moment of truth," said Jean-Paul. "The great plan is nearing completion. Soon I will give you your final instructions."

What was 'the great plan'? Jake thought frantically. It didn't sound good, but there was no time to worry about it now. The boy holding his left leg had loosened his grip slightly in his excitement as the 'game' flicked back to demo mode. This was his chance to escape. He lashed out with his foot and struck the boy hard on the cheek. The boy cried out in pain as Jake continued lashing his free foot wildly. He managed to get an arm free as well. The boys struggled to secure him but now Jake was swinging wildly with all available limbs, and anyone that got in his way soon regretted it. Before long he was free and sprinting out of the park.

Jake took a quick look behind him as he exited the park. Not only were the boys chasing him, but also a significant portion of the crowd. He couldn't outrun them all, so he'd have to try to outmanoeuvre them. He darted down an alleyway, dragging over bins behind him to make it hard for his pursuers. Jake knew that they would probably catch him, but there was no way he was going to make it easy for them. He glanced back as they jumped the bins, only metres behind him.

At the end of the alley were the streetlights of a main road, though Jake wasn't sure he'd make it. Suddenly, to his surprise, a red sports car screeched to a halt at the end of the alley. The passenger door clicked open and a voice shouted, "Get in!"

Jake looked up and saw Sarah behind the wheel – he didn't need asking twice. With the mob only a metre behind him he dived headfirst through the door, but felt one of them grab at his foot.

"Hold on to something!" said Sarah as she stamped on the accelerator. Jake grabbed hold of the chair as the car lurched forward, pulling him free from his pursuer's grasp.

Jake swung himself into the car and breathed a massive sigh of relief. "Where did you come from?" he asked, with a mixture of relief and shock.

"When I noticed you were gone, I drove down to look for you in your home town," she said. "I saw you being chased and thought you needed a hand."

"Thanks," he said. "Are you allowed to drive a car?"

"Who's around to stop me?" she said casually, flashing him a mischievous grin, though soon her face fell as she looked out at the deserted streets and remembered why no one was about. "It got bad quickly, didn't it?" she added.

"It sure did," replied Jake.

Sarah shifted uncomfortably in her seat. "Listen, Jake, when I came to look for you, the first place I went to was your flat," she said. "I saw your mum."

"They've got her, haven't they?" said Jake. Sarah nodded grimly as Jake sighed and stared out of the window, the features of his home town speeding past. Everything seemed different now; all the life had gone out of the place.

"Listen, Jake," said Sarah, abruptly. "I need you to come back to the house. We can stop all this, I really believe that, but we can't do it without you. I think – "

"You don't have to convince me, Sarah," Jake interrupted, with a quiet determination in his voice. "Jean-Paul is going to pay!"

Sarah smiled as she slid the car into sixth gear and accelerated back to Cumbria.

9

WAKING THE WORLD

It was getting late by the time Sarah and Jake arrived at the manor house. On the way back, Jake had told Sarah about the announcements that Jean-Paul was making. The news that Jean-Paul was communicating directly with the hypnotised population worried her. As soon as they got back, Jake found himself standing in front of Sarah and the three other kids that he had run away from earlier that day.

He told them the whole story: how practically the entire population was under Jean-Paul's control and how the maniac's 'great plan' was about to be put into action. They didn't like it any better than Sarah did.

For a long time they sat in stunned silence until Chun Mai finally spoke. "This is awful! Who does he think he is?" she said, pacing angrily. "Great plan?" she said, practically spitting the words out. "All those people had plans too. They planned to raise their kids, do their jobs, build lives for themselves. What makes him think that his plan is better?"

Chun Mai's words struck a chord deep within Jake. Going back to London had made him realise a few things. He saw everyone behaving in the same way, thinking the same way – and realised immediately how unnatural it all was. People were supposed to be individuals, they were supposed to be different. It was the differences that made life interesting. Jake frowned as he remembered all the time that he'd wasted trying to fit in, trying to be 'normal', when really there was no such thing. He was suddenly very angry with Jean-Paul for robbing all those people of their individuality, their personalities – for making the world a lifeless and boring place.

"I just wish we knew what it is that Jean-Paul's planning," said Alex.

"By the time we find that out, it'll be too late to stop him," said Jake. "We need to move now!"

"*We?*" said Chun Mai, her tone of voice calculated to remind Jake that not long ago he'd wanted nothing to do with any of them.

"Look, I'm sorry I ran, guys," said Jake. "But it's different now, I've seen what this man has done to the world and I want to help stop him!"

There was a long pause as the kids let his words sink in. Finally Alex broke the silence, "Then we're pleased to have you," he said. The kids nodded in agreement, even Robert. Despite the seriousness of the situation, Jake couldn't help grinning.

"He's got the whole world under his thumb," said Chun Mai returning to business. "How're we supposed to compete with that?"

"Come on, Chun Mai," said Sarah, "there must be a way."

"How?" asked Alex, desperately.

Sarah looked over at Robert. He had been uncharacteristically quiet since Jake had returned and right now he was deep in thought, not listening to the rest of the group.

"Robert," said Sarah. "What are you thinking?"

Robert didn't answer immediately; he was obviously working through something complex in his head. When he was finally ready, he opened his mouth to speak. "Jake," he said. "You're telling us that you saw Jean-Paul directly addressing people through the game?"

"Yes," replied Jake.

"That means that he can broadcast to the world's population whenever he likes."

"Probably," said Sarah.

"And I wouldn't mind betting that he's doing it from Razon HQ in Poland," added Robert.

"That would make sense," said Chun Mai.

Robert began to grin. "Well, guys, this changes everything!" he exclaimed, leaping to his feet.

"I don't understand," said Alex.

"I've been hypnotising people as part of my magic tricks since I was seven," he replied, "and I've become very good at it."

Sarah rolled her eyes. "Yeah, yeah, we know. You're a great magician, Robert – what's your point?"

Robert was annoyed by the interruption, but he soldiered on. "The point, Sarah, is that if someone can be hypnotised, they can also be un-hypnotised." He pointed theatrically at Chun Mai, "With my considerable expertise, and Chun Mai's programming skills, we could make an anti-brainwashing game that will break the trance. An antidote to Powerball!"

Sarah looked across at Chun Mai questioningly. "It's possible, I suppose," said Chun Mai, thoughtfully.

"Then all we'd have to do is broadcast it to the world," added Robert, triumphantly.

"From inside Razon's highly secure HQ, you mean?" questioned Jake.

"Okay, I admit getting into the place will be tough!" said Robert.

"Tough, but not impossible!" said Alex.

"You're right, we can do it!" said Sarah, looking around at the expressions of renewed optimism on the faces of her friends.

"I'm in," said Jake.

"Me too!" said Chun Mai.

"Cool!" said Alex, "We have a plan!"

The team spent the rest of that night, and the next day, working feverishly. Chun Mai and Robert were meticulously putting together a DVD of the antidote game, while Sarah and Jake tried to figure out how they would get into Razon HQ.

It was late at night before they were happy with the final plan. They agreed that it was best to wait until the morning to set off, and went to bed. However, not one of them could sleep. They all knew that the next day would not only be the most important of their lives, but probably the most important day in the history of the world.

10
THE Big Day

It was six o'clock when Jake awoke from a fitful sleep. He looked at the clock and yawned. He didn't need to be up for another half an hour but there was no way that he could stay in bed – he was far too nervous. He threw on a pair of trousers, a T-shirt and a zip-up jumper for the mission, and checked his rucksack: he had a map, a torch, a compass, a walkie-talkie and a copy of Robert and Chun Mai's antidote DVD. There wasn't much to forget, but still he checked it twice before going down to the kitchen to make a cup of tea.

As Jake flicked on the kettle, he heard Sarah walk into the kitchen. He turned to greet her, and saw instantly how worried she looked. He'd never seen her like this; Jake thought of her as a confident, strong character who would stand up to any danger.

"What if we fail?" she asked, sighing.

It was then that Jake realised that nobody is perfect. If Sarah, who spoke seven languages and thought nothing of staging daring rescue missions in borrowed sports cars, could suffer from a lack of confidence, then anyone could. Suddenly, Jake felt better about his own doubts and realised that it was his job to make Sarah feel better about hers.

"I guess we'd better not," he said. She laughed nervously. "Honestly though mate, umm, Sarah, I can't think of anyone I'd rather be going on a dangerous mission to save the world with than you." He blushed slightly as he tried to reassure her.

"Right back at you," she replied, the smile returning to her face. "Right, let's get ready." Her confidence had returned. The old Sarah was back.

By seven o'clock, the whole group had gathered in the field behind the manor house. Alex was busy preparing the remaining hoverpod for takeoff, and there was a mix of excitement and nervousness in the air. The kids shifted uncomfortably, waiting to set off.

Only Sarah, Jake and Robert were going to the Razon HQ. Chun Mai and Alex were to stay behind to provide technical support for the mission.

Alex clapped his oily hands together and slammed the engine cover of the hoverpod shut. He beamed at the rest of the group. "She's ready to fly," he said.

"Before we go: Chun Mai, Robert, are you sure

your anti-brainwashing game will work?" asked Sarah.

"Of course it'll work," said Robert. "Powerball is no match for my powers!" he boasted. Chun Mai jabbed him in the ribs. "Ow! Sorry, *our* powers."

"Well, let's just hope that your extreme cockiness is justified," said Sarah.

"Isn't it always?" replied Robert, smugly.

"I guess we'd better get going," said Sarah, swiftly changing the subject so she didn't have to answer.

"Hang on!" said Alex. "I almost forgot, I've got one more little toy for you!"

Alex pulled a device out of his pocket. It looked like a large remote control but it had a sharp metal hook on the front.

"What is it?" asked Jake.

"It's a grappling hook," Alex replied. "For scaling walls and swinging over obstructions! Would you like a demonstration?"

"Please," said Sarah, still not completely sure what he was talking about.

Alex smiled. He pressed a button and the metal hook fired out. It was attached to a metal wire. The hook embedded itself in the front wall of the barn.

"Tally ho!" said Alex as he jumped and swung through the door of the barn.

The kids winced as they heard a loud crash from inside. A few moments later, Alex hobbled out of the barn and the team breathed a sigh of relief.

"Any questions?" said Alex, clearly in some pain.

The kids looked at each other dubiously, and shook their heads as Alex silently handed them each a handful of grappling hooks.

"We'll be monitoring you the whole way," said Chun Mai. "Contact us on the walkie-talkies if you need anything," she said.

"I'm sure we will," said Jake.

They gave each other brief, nervous hugs, wished each other good luck, and soon Sarah, Robert and Jake were left alone with the hoverpod.

"Let's go," said Sarah as she clambered into the back seat.

Jake nodded and started to climb into the passenger seat, but Robert stopped him.

"Look, Jake," said Robert, shifting uncomfortably. "I wanted to say something to you." Robert paused trying to find the words. "Basically, umm, what I'm getting at is..."

"He's trying to apologise," interrupted Sarah from inside the hoverpod.

"Yeah," said Robert, "I'm sorry I gave you such a hard time before. You deserve to be here."

"Thanks," said Jake, surprised to be hearing this from his erstwhile enemy.

"So how about you drive the hoverpod?" said Robert. "You're better at it than me anyway."

Jake nodded and slapped Robert on the shoulder. He knew how hard it must have been for Robert to apologise. He clambered into the driver's seat. "Permission to launch?" he said into the radio.

"Roger, Jake, permission granted," said Alex over

the radio. Jake pressed the ignition button and soon the hoverpod was in the air.

The distance from the manor house to Razon HQ was just under a thousand miles. Nobody felt like talking; they were all concentrating on the task at hand. The only words spoken throughout the whole trip were from Sarah, half-heartedly pointing out landmarks as they flew over Germany. On another day this would have been fascinating, but right now all Jake could think about was how empty the city streets of Berlin and Dresden seemed as they passed overhead. He hadn't even bothered to turn on the camouflage function on the hoverpod.

Soon they were in Polish airspace. "Fly low, Jake," said Alex over the radio. "You're less likely to be picked up on radar that way."

Jake turned on the camouflage and pointed the joystick forwards. Soon he was zipping just above the rooftops of Polish cities. It was pretty scary stuff; every time a power cable or chimney stack rushed by, the kids winced collectively. After a while, the landscape became less urban and all they saw was grass, farmland and the occasional hill.

"Look on the bright side – at least the cows haven't been hypnotised," said Robert as they passed over a herd. Everyone laughed.

Their high spirits were short-lived, as their laughter was interrupted by a giant grey building looming in the distance and dominating the horizon. It was a huge, rectangular block that looked entirely out of place amongst all the greenery. A red light flashed up on the radar as they approached.

"That's it," said Sarah.
"Ugly thing, isn't it?" said Robert.

Jake climbed steeply until he was above the building and then set the hoverpod down on the roof. He turned off the engine and the kids crept out.

"Chun Mai," said Jake into his walkie-talkie, "have we been noticed?"

Back at the manor house, Chun Mai had hacked into the Razon system again and was monitoring activity inside the building. She had access to security cameras, emails, phone calls...little could go on in that building without Chun Mai knowing about it. She did a quick scan and responded, "No security alerts have been triggered, looks like you're okay for now."

In the middle of the roof was a large glass panel, through which the kids could see the inner workings of the building.

Razon HQ was made up of a large rectangular open space, around which fifteen floors of offices and other rooms were built. The kids could see all the goings-on on each floor, all the way down to the central courtyard. The building was a hive of activity. A number of serious-looking men and women in suits moved quickly around each floor and, more worryingly for the kids, there were also several beefy guards, each one carrying a rifle.

"Chun Mai, what are our entry options?" said Sarah into her walkie-talkie.

"Not sure," responded Chun Mai. "If you tried to get in through the roof you'd be spotted in three seconds flat. You'd also set off about ten different security alarms."

Sarah sighed; it didn't look good. Suddenly Jake had an idea.

"Maybe that's what we *want*," said Jake.

"What do you mean?" said Chun Mai.

"Alarms," said Jake. "Does the building have a fire alarm system?"

"Of course," said Chun Mai.

"Set it off – once everyone's been evacuated, we'll drop in through the ceiling. All the other alarms will be drowned out by the first one."

"Good idea," said Sarah.

"I agree," said Chun Mai. "Give me a second."

The kids waited and soon the muffled sound of a fire alarm could be heard through the glass. Quick as a flash, Sarah produced a screwdriver and began unscrewing a large panel of the glass from the roof. When she had loosened all the screws, she carefully slid the panel across and peered inside.

Robert peeked over the side of the building and saw the steadily growing number of employees gathering outside for the fire drill. "Is the building empty?" he said into his walkie-talkie.

"Yes," came the response from Chun Mai, "but it'll only last for another minute or so."

"We'd better get going then," said Robert.

The kids produced their grappling hooks, fired

them into the surface of the roof and attached the handles to the hooks on their belts.

"Hold on tight," said Sarah as they all lowered themselves through the open panel.

They dropped steadily into the belly of the building. They had got as far as the fifth floor down when the fire alarm stopped abruptly.

"That's not good," said Robert.

Chun Mai's urgent voice came across their walkie-talkies. "The alarm ended early, I don't know why, but you have to get out of sight – now!"

"Quick everyone, swing!" said Sarah and the three kids wiggled and squirmed to make the wires move. With every swing of the wires, they got closer to the railing along the edge of the tenth floor. They were within touching distance when they saw the first Razon employees filing back in.

I hope they don't look up, thought Jake, as he managed to get a foothold on the ledge and pull himself over. He quickly helped the others to do the same and the kids pressed the 'Retract' button on the handles. The wires retracted back up into their plastic cases embedded in the roof, scraping against the railing as they went. If it hadn't been for the hustle and bustle of the returning employees, someone would surely have heard.

Jake looked at a lift opposite him. He could see on the dial that someone was coming up: seventh floor, eighth floor…they would be with them in seconds.

"We need to hide," he said. "Now!"

11

ROBERTO'S 'GREAT IDEA'

"Phew," said Jake, as he stood bolt upright against the wall, "that was close."

In the nick of time they had found an empty office and were currently making themselves as flat as they could, with their backs to one of the walls, so that they were out of the view of the room's security camera.

"So, we're in," said Sarah. "What next?"

"We need to get out of this room," said Jake, as the security camera moved slightly and the kids were forced to edge sideways like crabs to remain in its blind spot. "Don't ask me how, though," he continued.

"Well," said Robert, "it's lucky for you two that I have a plan then, isn't it?" He lifted his walkie-talkie to his mouth. "Chun Mai, I need you to disable the security cameras."

"Okay, can do," said Chun Mai, and, with a couple of well-chosen keystrokes, she plunged Razon's CCTV technicians into deep confusion as their screens simultaneously went blank. "But whatever you're going to do, do it quickly," she added. "Security will be freaking out! Eventually they'll work out what I've done and they'll undo it."

"Okay, let's go," said Robert, opening the door.

"We can't just walk out!" said Sarah. "They may not have security cameras any more, but the guards still have eyes."

"And guns!" added Jake.

"Relax, guys," said Robert, "I can deal with the guards, just trust me."

In the absence of a better plan, Sarah and Jake took a deep breath and followed Robert out of the door. As predicted, within about six steps they were stopped by a guard. The intimidating man towered over them, his face a mixture of rage and surprise.

"What're you kids doing?" he asked.

"That's a reasonable question," said Robert, coolly producing a gold pocket watch. "And one that you deserve to have the answer to," he added, swinging the watch gently in front of the guard's face. "But first, concentrate on the watch."

The guard immediately began blinking distractedly. "What are you—"

"When I snap my fingers you will be under my control!" said Robert loudly, flinging his arms up as if he were on stage. He waited a moment and then

115

clicked his fingers. The expression on the guard's face changed dramatically. All the menace faded and was replaced by a blank stare – he looked a lot like a Powerball player.

"You will lead us to the main control room," said Robert. "If anyone tries to stop us, you will tell them that we are Jean-Paul's children and you are giving us a tour of the facility. Do you understand?"

"I understand," replied the guard, as he turned around and began walking.

"Okay," said Sarah. "That was impressive."

"I thank you," said Robert, grinning and performing a miniature bow.

They followed the guard down some stairs and along a corridor.

Every time they passed a Razon employee they got a funny look, but thanks to their armed escort everyone assumed that they were supposed to be there.

Their luck soon ran out though, when another guard approached them. This one had a slightly darker uniform and three stripes on his right arm. The kids assumed that he was of higher rank than the one that they had chosen as their guide.

"What's going on here?" he said.

"These are Jean-Paul's children," said the first guard, in a low, monotone voice. "I'm giving them a tour of the —"

"Jean-Paul doesn't have any children!" the second guard interrupted.

Quickly, Robert produced his pocket watch and dangled it in front of the second guard's face. The guard angrily batted it out of his hand.

"Oh dear," said Robert, as the watch smashed against a wall.

"Enough messing about," said the guard. "What're you kids doing here?"

They looked at each other, unsure of what to say. Suddenly, Sarah kicked the guard in the shin as hard as she could.

"Run!" she yelled, as the guard cried out in pain.

WHAT HAPPENS NEXT? YOU DECIDE...

**Jake makes
a wise choice**
turn to page 120

**An impossible
choice**
turn to page 126

jake makes a wise choice

The kids ran as if their lives depended on it – which they did. They saw with a quick glance behind them that it would take more than a kick from a twelve-year-old to stop the guard who was bearing down on them fast. Sarah saw the door of a lift slide open up ahead, and a group of Razon workers get out.

"Quick, in here!" she shouted, and the kids ducked through the crowd to get into the lift.

"Chun Mai!" shouted Jake into his walkie-talkie. "What floor is the main control room on?"

"Four," responded Chun Mai.

Jake hammered on the '4' button and the doors began to close, clicking shut just as the guard slammed into them. His furious red face pressed up against the glass as they began to move downwards.

The guard must have triggered an alarm, because the air was suddenly filled with a high-pitched ringing. Through the glass, they could see more guards streaming out of doors on the lower floors of the building. A group of four burly guards hustled into another lift to follow them.

"Chun Mai, I need you to disable the lift on the southern side of the building!" shouted Sarah into her walkie-talkie.

Chun Mai did as she was told, and the kids saw the guards in the other lift shouting as they ground to halt. She had bought them a little time, but it wouldn't be long before other guards started running up the stairs.

"When you get out of the lift, turn left and then right, you can't miss it," directed Chun Mai.

As they reached the fourth floor, they piled out of the lift and ran. After the right turn that Chun Mai had advised they saw a large, heavy door.

"That must be the control room!" said Sarah. "Robert, wait at the end of the corridor and tell us if anyone's coming."

With Robert on lookout, Sarah and Jake ran to the door. Jake sighed as he realised that the room was protected by an electronic combination lock.

"Can you find out the entry code, Chun Mai?" said Sarah into the walkie-talkie.

"I think so," came the response.

Chun Mai took a deep breath and began tapping furiously at her keyboard. She would need to hack deep into the Razon network to find the code.

After a couple of wrong turns she found a document labelled 'Access'. She opened it.

Jake and Sarah waited nervously by the heavy door, willing Chun Mai to hurry. They knew that any minute now they would be discovered, and the tension was almost unbearable.

"I've got it!" said Chun Mai. "Two-four-seven-five-eight..." she recited. Jake punched in the numbers. As Chun Mai was about to read the final number the walkie-talkie crackled and fuzzed, before finally cutting out altogether.

"Hello, hello!" shouted Sarah, shaking the walkie-talkie frantically. "Chun Mai, come in!"

"It's broken!" said Jake, horrified. "How're we going to get the last number?"

Just then, Robert saw four guards emerge from a door marked 'Stairs', and begin opening all the doors along the corridor. It wouldn't be long before they rounded the corner and spotted them. He ducked out of sight and ran to Jake and Sarah.

"Come on, let's go, people are coming," he whispered, urgently.

"But we don't know the last digit of the code," barked Sarah.

"Just press anything!" said Robert, reaching for the number pad.

"No," said Jake grabbing Robert's hand. "If we get it wrong it could lock us out, and we wouldn't be able to try again!"

"So what do you suggest?" replied Robert.

"I can figure it out!" said Jake. From out of the blue, he'd remembered an article that he'd read by a man who cracked codes for a living. He racked his brains. It had said that when choosing a random sequence of numbers, people didn't tend to use the same number twice. Using this logic, Jake could eliminate two, four, five, seven and eight as possibilities. The article also said that people stayed away from the corners of number pads when choosing a code: in this case that also eliminated one, three and nine. With those numbers discarded, there was only one left. It wasn't a definite, but it was the most likely.

"Hey you!" said a guard from the end of the corridor.

Jake took a deep breath and pressed the number six. The red light on the lock turned green and the kids rushed inside, just managing to slam the door shut on the advancing guards.

The control room was large and white, the floor was tiled and there was no furniture except for a huge computer that whirred noisily at one end. There was a large camera attached to the top, presumably for Jean-Paul's broadcasts.

"If only Chun Mai could see this," said Robert, as the kids approached it.

Sarah clicked the 'Global Broadcast' key, and the screen was filled with the grinning face of Jean-Paul. He was laughing heartily.

"What's going on?" said Sarah.

"You didn't think it would be that easy, did you?" said Jean-Paul from the screen.

With a violent hiss, a white gas started spraying from the walls. As the kids breathed it in, they became instantly drowsy. Before long they had collapsed to the floor, fast asleep.

Now continue to page 131

an impossible choice

The kids pelted down the hallway, closely followed by a very angry guard.

"Split up," shouted Sarah. "He can't catch us all."

So they did. Sarah darted right, down a hallway, and Robert went left. Jake doubled back on himself, sliding neatly past the guard and leaving him with no idea which way to turn. Angrily, the guard grabbed his walkie-talkie.

"Intruder alert!" he shouted.

Moments later, a loud high-pitched alarm rang out all around the building. Guards began pouring out of doors left, right and centre. When Sarah found her way blocked by three of them she realised that she would have to take evasive action. She fired a grappling hook into the main roof of the building and swung across the open space to the other side.

As she neared the other side, the wire slipped

from her grasp. Sarah managed to grab hold of the ledge and looked down in horror at the lethal nine-storey drop below. She struggled desperately to get a firmer grip, and eventually managed to haul herself up, over the railing and on to the floor on the other side, breathing a deep sigh of relief.

Her relief was short lived. There were even more guards on this side. When she picked herself up, she found five guns pointed straight at her. She sighed and put her hands up in surrender.

Robert didn't fare much better. The hallway he ran down had a troop of guards in it; he tried to turn back but found his way blocked by yet more guards.

"I guess you've caught me," he said. "Or have you?" he added mysteriously, pulling a smoke bomb out of his pocket. "Allakazam!" he cried, and disappeared in a puff of smoke.

Unfortunately, the room Robert disappeared into was a small cleaning cupboard. It didn't take the guards long to figure out where he'd gone, and they soon found him hiding between the mops and the paper towels.

Jake was luckier. He managed to get to the fourth floor and found an unattended sandwich cart outside an office. He peered round a door and saw the sandwich seller inside chatting with one of the employees. He glanced at the cart: it was big and had a rubbish compartment at the bottom.

There was just about enough space for him to hide.

He climbed into the compartment, tucking himself into a tight ball. It wasn't long before the cart began moving. "This darn thing gets heavier every day," he heard the sandwich seller muttering as they set off.

Eventually, he heard the sandwich seller speak again. "Lunch!" he called in a loud voice. Jake peered round the edge of the trolley and saw people emerging to select their sandwiches, crisps and cakes.

Jake didn't know for sure that the room they had left was empty, but he would have to take the risk. Quick as a flash, he burst out of the cart and ran inside, slamming the door behind him. The door was secured by an electronic combination lock; quickly, he changed the combination using the panel on the inside. With the staff safely locked out, he finally turned to find himself in the control room.

The room was very large and white. The floor was tiled and there was no furniture except for a huge computer that whirred noisily at one end of the room. There was a large camera attached to the top of it used, Jake assumed, for Jean-Paul's evil global broadcasts.

Jake approached the computer. There was a button on the keyboard labelled 'Global Broadcast'. He pressed it and a box came up on the screen, asking him whether he wanted to broadcast live or play a DVD. He clicked 'Play DVD' and swiftly pulled the antidote game from his bag.

Suddenly, Jean-Paul's face appeared at the top of the screen. Jake took a step back, shocked.

"I wouldn't do that if I were you," said Jean-Paul from the screen.

"Oh yeah, why not?" asked Jake.

The camera panned round to reveal Robert and Sarah tied up and gagged. Jake sighed; he knew what was coming next.

"Simple. Because if you do, I'll kill your friends!" replied Jean-Paul.

Jake was so close to ending Jean-Paul's reign of terror. All he had to do was slide in the antidote DVD, but he couldn't. He couldn't live with the deaths of his friends on his conscience. He looked down at the DVD and then back at the terrified faces of Sarah and Robert on the screen.

"Be a good boy and snap that DVD!" said Jean-Paul. "Do that and you'll all be safe, I promise."

Jake growled angrily and snapped the DVD. He sank to the floor with his head in his hands.

"Weak child!" laughed Jean-Paul, as two guards battered down the door of the control room.

12

jean-Paul's new World Order

Jake sat forlornly somewhere in the Razon building. To his right were Robert and Sarah. None of them were tied up, but there were two stern looking guards at the door, watching their every move. The room was silent; nobody felt much like talking. The human race was doomed to eternal slavery and there was nothing left that they could do about it.

Jake looked around at the room where they were being kept. It was strange, almost like a cinema. It had a massive screen at one end and five rows of seats. In front of the screen was a small stage.

Suddenly, the doors burst open. The guards got out of the way quickly as Jean-Paul strode through the room and took his place on the stage. A projector at the back of the room began whirring and a huge image of Jean-Paul's face filled the screen behind him. This man had one giant ego!

Jean-Paul gazed at his captives and smiled. He began clapping.

"Well done, my friends," he said. "Very well done, I'm impressed. Of course, you didn't have a hope of actually succeeding but hey, no one else has even tried to stop me. It's all been a bit too easy, to be honest." The grin on his face made the kids feel sick with hatred. "I expected more resistance but none came – once the game took hold of the youngsters, the rest fell like dominoes!"

"Why are you doing this?" shouted Sarah, losing her cool completely.

"That's a good question, young lady," said Jean-Paul. "But before I answer it, let me ask you one. You're obviously a confident, capable girl. Do you like to get your own way?"

"What do you mean?" growled Sarah, through gritted teeth.

"When these boys do what you say, it makes you feel good doesn't it? You love being in charge, you love how important it makes you feel, don't you?"

"No," said Sarah, "I just want to save the world from madmen like you!"

"Darling," said Jean-Paul, "if I'm mad, then so is the rest of the world. Everyone likes to feel important, everyone enjoys power. I've just taken it to the next level." He threw his hands into the air. "I'm the most powerful man in the world! I am a God!"

"You're deluded, more like!" said Jake.

Jean-Paul's face fell. He walked over to Jake and leant in so that his face was only centimetres away. "That is a very stupid thing to say, my boy," he said. "I don't think you realise who you're dealing with, do you?" He leant back and began to shout. "I can destroy entire continents as easily as turning off a light switch, I can do whatever I want!"

"So what?" said Robert.

"Pardon me?" replied Jean-Paul.

"So...what?" repeated Robert slowly, as if he was explaining something to a toddler. "We're not scared of you – and we're not impressed," he added, coolly. "So just do what you're going to do or leave us alone!"

Jean-Paul paused. The kids all held their breath as they waited to see what he was going to do. Suddenly, to their surprise, he burst out laughing. "You kids are priceless!" he said. "Such spirit! I'm going to enjoy working with you."

"What?" said Sarah. "We'll never help you! You must be joking."

"Not only will you help me," said Jean-Paul, "you'll be a vital part of the next phase of my plan!"

"What's that?" said Jake. He'd seen enough James Bond movies to know that villains always explain their full plan when they think they've won.

"I'm going to start the biggest war the world has ever seen!" Jean-Paul said, triumphantly. The kids sat flabbergasted; he couldn't be serious. "Soon I will give the order for the president of the USA, your British Prime Minister and several other European leaders to attack China. The Chinese will, of course, retaliate. Then, having given the world a little push in the right direction, I will snap the world out of its trance and the rest will take care of itself."

Jean-Paul smiled contentedly. "The first truly global war," he said, misty-eyed. "Just imagine it."

Sarah stood up angrily. "You fool, you fool!" she shouted as she charged towards Jean-Paul. "Think of all the people you'll kill!" She tried feebly to kick and punch Jean-Paul but he only laughed as the guards pulled her off him. "Why?" she shouted, as they dragged her back to her seat.

"Another excellent question," responded Jean-Paul. "I think you are the cleverest one of all," he continued, smiling at Sarah. "There are many reasons. One, of course, is money – naturally a world war is a good opportunity for a man like me to make a buck or two," he said, as if it was the most normal thing in the world, before pausing, deep in thought.

"But mainly," he continued, "the main reason is... because I can!" said Jean-Paul, with a mad glint in his eyes. "I'm looking forward to it, it's going to be fun," he added as he headed for the door triumphantly.

"We'll have no part in this, Jean-Paul. We'd rather die!" said Robert as Jean-Paul walked away.

"Believe me, that's not a problem to arrange," he responded. "But I'll let you think about it for a while. I'm confident that you'll reconsider!"

Jean-Paul left the room, followed by the guards. The door slammed shut and they heard the click of a lock. They slumped in their seats, desolate and defeated.

Just when they thought that it couldn't get any worse, the lights dimmed and the image of Jean-Paul's face began to fade. Soon the blue-grey moving shapes of Powerball were being projected in its place; it was a non-playable demo version, but it was no less addictive to those watching it.

The kids tried everything not to get sucked in. They tried to smash the projector but it was behind bulletproof glass. They tried closing their eyes and covering their ears but they couldn't block out the sound. Slowly but surely they began to fall under the spell of the game.

Jake looked at Robert. He was already gone. His eyes were glazed over and he was transfixed by the moving images on the screen.

"Goodbye, Jake," said Sarah, drowsily. "It was great knowing you."

"No, Sarah! You've got to fight it," shouted Jake, but, in truth, he was getting sleepier by the second, and finding it harder and harder to tear his eyes away from the screen.

A few minutes later no one was talking. They all just sat there, silently watching the moving shapes on the gigantic screen.

NOW CHOOSE YOUR ENDING!

Techies to the rescue
turn to page 138

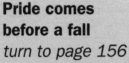

Pride comes before a fall
turn to page 156

Grown-ups are good for something
turn to page 172

Techies to the rescue

part one

Back at the manor house, Chun Mai and Alex sat helplessly, watching security camera footage from the Razon Building. They looked on in horror as their friends slowly fell under Jean-Paul's spell.

"I can't look at this any more!" said Chun Mai, switching off the screens.

"What're we going to do?" asked Alex, hoping that Chun Mai had some idea, some miraculous plan to save the day. She didn't.

"I don't know," said Chun Mai, her voice cracking as she fought back tears. "The whole plan's ruined, just flushed down the toilet!"

Alex sat up straight, the beginnings of an idea forming in his mind. "That's it!" said Alex.

"What?" replied Chun Mai.

"Flushed down the toilet!" said Alex.

"You're going to have to explain further," said Chun Mai, trying to decide whether or not Alex had finally lost the plot.

"Have you got a blueprint of the Razon building on the computer?" asked Alex, excitedly.

"Of course I have!"

"Let me see."

Chun Mai still wasn't sure where Alex was going with this but she did as she was told.

"There," she said. "Now, please explain!"

"Look at that!" said Alex pointing to the bottom of the blueprint. "Sewers! I don't know why I didn't think of it before. That's a way in! Look, the main sewage channel goes right up into the basement of the building."

Chun Mai studied the blueprint carefully. He was right, there was a very small underground tunnel that they could probably just about fit through.

"That's strange," she said.

"Not really," said Alex, "Razon HQ is built on the site of an old sewage works, remember."

"Okay, Alex," she said. "So we can get inside. What do we do then?"

"We rescue the others and then broadcast the antidote game," he replied.

"How?"

"Well, okay, that's the one tiny detail I haven't yet figured out!"

Chun Mai took a deep breath and stood up. She picked up a pen from the table and began twirling it between her fingers. Alex smiled. Whenever she did that it meant she was thinking something through, and when Chun Mai started thinking, good things happened. She was one of the cleverest people that Alex had ever met and right now he could almost hear the cogs turning in her brain.

"The obvious thing to do is to try to wake up the others and then storm the control room as a group of five," she said, pacing around the room. "Though that requires us getting from the basement to the screening room without being seen," she added. "Doesn't seem that likely, does it?"

"No," replied Alex. "Especially as we'll stink from our walk in the sewers!"

"Quite," said Chun Mai, working the pen through her fingers furiously as she tried to piece together a plan. She took a long look at the blueprint and a smile began to cross her face. "Getting to this room is a much more realistic target," she said, as she pointed to a room just above the basement.

"What's in there?" asked Alex.

Chun Mai tapped some keys and brought up the security camera footage of the room. "Oh, not much," she said, moving the camera to show Alex the whole room. "Some boxes, a broken photocopier, a couple of tables – but, most importantly, a computer!" Chun Mai grinned as the plan came together in her head. She turned to Alex. "If I can get to a computer inside the building, one that's actually part of the Razon network, I think I might be able to..."

"What?" said Alex. He couldn't bear the suspense.

"I might be able to hack into the main control room computer!" she said, barely able to contain her excitement. "We could broadcast the antidote DVD without being anywhere near the control room!"

"That's great stuff," said Alex. "What about the others, though?"

"When everyone at Razon realises we've undone all their hard work, they'll freak out!" said Chun Mai, grinning at all the chaos she was going to unleash. "Amongst the confusion, we'll stand a better chance of getting to the screening room and saving them."

"You're right," said Alex. "They'll be too busy to worry about us!"

With not a moment to lose, the kids ran out to Alex's barn, where he was working on the damaged hoverpod. They looked at the battered machine and wondered whether it was up to taking them three quarters of the way across Europe.

"Will it fly?" asked Chun Mai, sceptically.

"It should," said Alex, unsure.

"What do you mean, it *should*?" asked Chun Mai.

"Well, I haven't had a chance to test it yet," he replied, defensively.

"Sewers, death-trap flying machines...this mission just gets better and better," Chun Mai sighed. "Well, no time to test it now."

The pair pushed the hoverpod out of the hangar, clambered aboard and strapped themselves in. Taking a deep breath, Alex pressed the ignition button. The engine spluttered and coughed but he eventually managed to get it into the air.

"Come on, Bessie," said Alex to the hoverpod, as he battled with the engine to keep climbing.

"Bessie?" said Chun Mai, raising her eyebrows.

"Yeah, I name all my inventions," said Alex. "What's wrong with that?"

"Oh, nothing," replied Chun Mai, stifling a grin. "Totally normal!"

When they eventually reached the optimum height, Alex ignited the thrusters and they were on their way.

"That's a relief," said Chun Mai.

"Now let's just hope we get there in one piece," said Alex.

"What do you mean?" replied Chun Mai.

"Well, there's a very small chance the engine will blow up in mid-air," said Alex matter-of-factly. "But I wouldn't worry about it."

"You really know how to make a person feel at ease, Alex," said Chun Mai, whilst nervously eyeing the hard ground below them.

It was getting dark when the hoverpod spluttered

and struggled to its destination. In the failing light they could just about see Razon HQ in the distance.

"According to the blueprint, there should be a manhole cover around here somewhere," said Alex.

The pair searched through the tall grass with torches for nearly twenty minutes before they finally uncovered the circle of rusty metal hidden amongst the moss and leaves. Alex set about opening it. It was stiff, and hadn't been touched for years, but eventually he managed to prise it open.

The pair gazed down into the murky darkness of the sewer, neither of them particularly happy about going in. Alex opened a holdall that he had brought from the hoverpod and fished out two pairs of what looked like giant wellies.

"These are called waders," he said. "I found them in one of the empty rooms back at the manor house. I think they're normally for fishing, but they'll do the job." He handed a pair to Chun Mai and she pulled them on, reluctantly.

They both looked over the edge and frowned. "Oh, you might want this as well," Alex added, handing Chun Mai a clothes peg.

"What's this for?" she asked.

"Your nose," replied Alex, with a grin.

Clipping their nostrils together with the clothes pegs, they swung over the edge of the manhole and splashed down into the sewage water. They drudged through, the foul water almost breaching the top of their waders as they went. Even though they were wearing the clothes pegs, the smell was awful. The air was thick with the stench and it was pitch black.

"Do you know where you're going?" asked Chun Mai, trying not to gag.

"As long as we keep heading north, we'll be fine," Alex said. "Just don't touch the walls, there's stuff down here that you really don't want on your hands."

"Okay," said Chun Mai.

"And watch out for sewer rats, I bet they're as big as dogs down here!"

"Alex?" said Chun Mai.

"Yes," he replied.

"Stop talking."

Finally, they reached a section that Alex recognised from the blueprint. "The basement should be just above us," he said, climbing up a long ladder built into the wall.

A few minutes later they had clambered up into the basement of the Razon HQ. They eagerly pulled off their waders and vowed never to go anywhere near a sewer ever again.

TeCHieS TO THe reSCUe parT TWO

As predicted, getting to the small office was not hard. It was in a part of the building that was rarely used. Chun Mai and Alex were able to creep undetected from the basement to the room with no fuss at all.

Whilst Alex kept watch through the glass panel in the office door, Chun Mai got to work. After attaching one of her laptops to the Razon computer and loading up some of her custom-designed hacking programmes, she gained access to the Razon system. Unfortunately, hacking into the main control room computer was taking longer than she'd thought.

She kept tapping away at the keys, frantically trying different ways to access the computer, but, whatever she tried, failed. The system was far too complex and too well designed to get into, at least with the equipment and time she had. After an hour, Alex began to get worried.

"How're you doing over there?" he asked.

Chun Mai laid her head against the desk and sighed. "I'm sorry, Alex," she said. "I can't do it, the system's too good. Cracking it would take days."

"We don't have days," Alex pointed out.

"Yes, Alex, I know," snapped Chun Mai, more angry at herself than at him.

"Is there anything we can do?" he asked.

Chun Mai looked at the screens and thought hard for a moment. A backup plan had actually occurred to her about twenty minutes ago, but it was hugely dangerous. She wanted to avoid it at all costs, but, right now, she simply couldn't think of another way to save the others and also broadcast the antidote.

"Well, there is one thing," she said. "Razon have installed a self-destruct function in the building, I guess just in case they need to destroy the evidence of what they're doing here. If I trigger it, the whole place will blow up after five minutes."

"That doesn't sound great," said Alex.

"I know," she said. "But it's our only hope. If everyone's evacuating, they won't have time to worry about us. We'll be able to broadcast the antidote DVD and free the others."

"And get out alive?" asked Alex, doubtfully.

"If we're quick enough," said Chun Mai.

Alex stood, frowning. It was incredibly risky but as he racked his brain for an alternative he couldn't for the life of him think of one.

"We won't do it if you don't want to," said Chun Mai. "We have to agree one hundred per cent."

Alex thought carefully. "Okay, if we have to," he said eventually.

"Right," said Chun Mai, "set your watch. From the moment I press 'Enter', we'll have exactly five minutes. You get the guys, and I'll broadcast the message."

Chun Mai took a deep breath, typed frantically, and then sprang out of her chair, before finally pressing the 'Enter' key.

"Here goes," gulped Alex, as the kids sprinted out of the room. "Good luck!"

Jean-Paul was in the main control room, preparing to address the President of the USA, when the alarms began to ring. An electronic voice came across the intercom, "Warning! Self-destruct sequence initiated. Detonation in five minutes."

Jean-Paul turned angrily to his chief technician. "What is going on?" he boomed.

"I'm sorry, Sir, it's the auto-destruct sequence – it's been triggered!"

"I can see that, now un-trigger it!" said Jean-Paul.

"I can't," said the technician. "It's not letting me, someone must have hacked into the system!"

"Impossible!" shouted Jean-Paul, angrily. Throwing the technician out of the way, he began frantically tapping at keys. The technician picked himself up and headed for the door, as did the rest of the staff in the room, but Jean-Paul stayed, desperately trying to undo what Chun Mai had done.

"Nooo!" he roared, as he realised that there was nothing he could do.

"Detonation in four minutes," intoned the frustratingly calm electronic voice.

Jean-Paul realised that it was time to run. "Start the helicopter!" he barked into his walkie-talkie.

"Yes, Sir!" said a voice from the other end.

Jean-Paul stormed into the hallway. Amongst the flurry of people rushing to get out, he saw one small figure coming the other way. It was Chun Mai.

"You!" he thundered. Chun Mai froze, and then tried to run past him into the control room. He grabbed her. "You've got something to do with those kids, haven't you? This is your doing!"

Chun Mai was more scared than she had been in her whole life, but she stood her ground and looked Jean-Paul straight in the eye. "Yes!" she said, "and I've never been more proud of anything I've done."

Jean-Paul's face exploded with rage. "You little – "

"Detonation in three minutes," came the electronic voice.

"You don't have the time to waste on me right now!" exclaimed Chun Mai.

Jean-Paul glared at her furiously, but he knew she was right. He let go of her. "This isn't over!" he said, as he turned and ran for the helicopter pad.

"I sincerely hope not," said Chun Mai, as she ran into the control room. She pulled the DVD out of her bag and placed it in the main computer's DVD drive. She hammered the 'Global Broadcast' button and the antidote game began to play.

She did a final check to make sure that the game was running properly and sprinted out of the door, with little over two minutes to avoid being blown up.

Alex wasn't doing quite so well. He had found the room where the kids were being kept but was having trouble getting in. He barged the door with his shoulder, kicked it, even threw things at it, but it wasn't budging. The building was empty now – everyone had escaped, and Alex was aware that he was running out of time.

"Detonation in two minutes."

Alex took a deep breath and closed his eyes. He couldn't panic; he needed to think. With his brain more relaxed, an idea quickly formed. Armed with his trusty screwdriver, he unfastened the front panel of the door's digital lock, revealing the electronics inside. He pulled out his mobile phone and broke it against the floor. He ripped out two wires, exposing the metal inside, and held them up to the lock's microchip. With a flash and a puff of smoke, the lock short-circuited and the door opened.

"Why didn't I do that to begin with?" asked Alex out loud to himself as he rushed inside.

The antidote DVD was already playing inside the screening room, thanks to Chun Mai, and the other kids were starting to wake up.

"Alex?" said Jake. "What're you doing here?"

Alex was about to explain when Chun Mai's voice came blaring out of his walkie-talkie. "Alex, where are you?" she shouted.

"We're just coming now!" he replied.

"You'll never make it out in time!" she cried. Alex looked at his watch. She was right; they had less than a minute. It would never be enough.

"Hang on," said Chun Mai. "I've got an idea! Lean out of the window."

"Why?"

"Just do it!" she yelled.

Chun Mai sprinted round to the east side of the building where Alex was leaning out of the window, desperately waving. She pulled the grappling hook out of her bag and fired. The hook embedded itself in the wall next to Alex's head.

She swiftly fastened her end of the metal wire to a nearby tree. "Quick! Slide down!" she shouted into her walkie-talkie.

Sarah was the first to go. She took off her jumper, folded it into a loop and hooked it over the wire.

"I hope this holds," she said as she slid down the wire. Jake and Robert followed her example, then finally Alex slid down as the electronic voice began counting down. "Ten, nine, eight..."

"Run!" yelled Alex, as soon as he hit the ground.

They didn't need to be told twice! They sprinted away as fast as they could. Seconds later, a thunderous blast threw them into the air. Everything went dark as dust and rubble blotted out the sun.

Some time later, Alex opened his eyes. Through the clearing

dust and debris in the air he could see only the bare foundations of Razon HQ. Nothing else was left. He'd seen plenty of explosions in his time but never one this massive; it was breathtaking.

"Is everyone okay?" he asked. He breathed a sigh of relief as he saw his friends slowly haul themselves to their feet. They each looked at the space where Razon HQ had been, taking in what had just happened.

Then, in unison, they silently turned and walked away from the wreckage.

After walking for about an hour, they reached a small village. A broad smile stretched across each of their faces as they saw the population wandering about the main high street. They were pretty confused, but they were free.

"We did it!" said Sarah, as the kids erupted into ecstatic cheers. They jumped around, high fived, whooped and cheered.

"I just wish Jean-Paul hadn't escaped," said Alex, when everyone had calmed down.

At this, Chun Mai smiled and pulled out her palmtop. The display showed a small red dot moving slowly across a map of Belarus. "I had a run-in with him earlier," she explained. "I managed to plant a tracking device on him. Anywhere Jean-Paul goes, we'll know."

"Well done," said Robert, hugely impressed.

"Yeah," said Sarah. "Now that's what I call thinking on your feet."

"Cheers, guys," said Chun Mai, flushing. "Come on, let's go home."

The next day, MI6, the Secret Intelligence Service, received a very interesting package. It contained a wealth of information on precisely what had been happening over the past weeks. It described how Jean-Paul had used Powerball to enslave the world and how close he had come to starting World War III. Most importantly, it also contained information on the precise wherabouts of Jean-Paul. Three days later, MI6 agents arrested him in Russia.

The package also let them know that there was a new crime-fighting force on the scene, and that that force was young, brave and ready for anything.

Around MI6 this mystery group became known simply as 'The M.I.Five'.

pride comes Before a fall

part one

Jake was almost lost to a hypnotic trance. He knew that the game was taking him but he wasn't going to go down without a fight. Keep focused, he told himself. He set himself maths puzzles, he thought about his mum's cookery, he thought about classic West Ham games, he thought about everything he loved – anything to slow the advance of the hypnosis.

After about twenty minutes Jake began to hear things, or at least he thought he did. Through the blaring noise of Powerball he thought he could hear Chun Mai's voice, though his brain was so confused that he didn't know whether it was real or not. The voice continued, however, and, as it became more insistent, he realised that it *was* real and that it was coming out of the intercom on the wall.

He summoned up all his concentration and listened.

"Guys!" said the voice from the wall. "It's Chun Mai. If any of you can hear me, raise your hand."

With extreme concentration Jake managed to move the tips of his fingers, then his whole hand, then his arm. With one final jerking movement, he raised his hand in the air as if he was answering a maths question in class.

Back at the manor house, Chun Mai and Alex cheered and hugged each other. Their message had got through! They had seen the kids falling under the spell of Powerball over Razon's security cameras. Jean-Paul had confiscated their walkie-talkies so Chun Mai had hacked into the company's intercom system and, after a bit of jiggery-pokery, managed to broadcast her voice to the room. Unfortunately, for everyone apart from Jake, it was too late.

"Jake," said Chun Mai, "we have a plan. Now listen carefully, I need you to get up."

Jake took a deep breath and stood up.

"Well done, Jake. Now move the table at the front of the room over to the corner."

Jake approached the front of the room. As he got closer to the screen, he began to get sucked in again. He started to watch the flashing shapes moving about on the screen with fascination.

"Jake!" screamed Chun Mai over the intercom, snapping him out of his trance. He took a breath, closed his eyes and dragged the table across the room to the corner. "Now, climb on the table," said Chun Mai.

It seemed a strange thing to ask him to do but he did as he was told.

"You should be able to see an air vent up ahead," said Chun Mai. "I want you to unscrew the panel on the front." Jake pulled a screwdriver out of his pocket and went to work. It took a while to get the thing off, especially as Jake was still partially hypnotised, but eventually the panel fell to the floor with a clang.

"Climb in, Jake. The main control room is just east of where you are. If you crawl through the air vents in that direction you should be able to drop down into it," said Chun Mai.

Even in his confused state, Jake saw a problem with this plan. He pulled out a piece of paper and a marker pen and wrote 'NO DVD!' in large black letters. He held his makeshift sign up to the security camera.

"No DVD?" said Chun Mai, turning to Alex. "What does that mean?"

Alex sighed. "Jean-Paul must have confiscated all of the antidote DVDs."

"I can't believe we didn't think of that!" said Chun Mai, shaking her head. "What do we do now?"

"Only one thing we can do!" said Alex, taking the microphone from Chun Mai.

As Jake waited for a response to his message, he

felt as if every fibre of his mind and body was telling him to turn around and watch the screen, all except the one tiny corner of his brain that knew what would happen if he did. Jake had to cling on to that tiny part – it represented his freedom, his only chance of not becoming a slave.

Alex's voice came through the intercom. "Jake," he said, "we only have one option left, and it's a long shot. You're going to have to try to break the hypnosis yourself. If you make a speech over the global broadcast system, reminding people of their lives before they were hypnotised, there's a small chance that some of them could snap out of the trance."

Jake wrote another sign and held it up to the camera. 'HOW SMALL?' it said.

"I'm not going to lie, Jake," said Alex. "It's very unlikely that it'll have an effect, but we have to try!" Jake nodded and, without a second thought, clambered into the air vent. "Good luck," added Alex.

The air vent was small and cramped. Jake crawled east as he was instructed, being careful not to make too much noise. The further away he crawled, the more the effects of the hypnosis seemed to wear off, and soon he was himself again. He breathed a sigh of relief.

The air vents were used to heat and cool the Razon building. For this reason there were many open sections in the metal passages. Jake would look through these every time he passed one, trying to get an idea of where he was. Eventually he glanced through one of the openings and was sure that he was over the main control room. There was only one problem: the room wasn't empty. A technician stood working at the main computer.

Luckily, Alex and Chun Mai could see the technician too, and they had a plan. After scrolling through the staff files on the Razon network, Chun Mai hacked into the intercom in the main control room and made an announcement.

"Would John Richardson come to office 2C immediately, please!" They crossed their fingers as they saw the technician sigh and head for the door.

Jake seized the opportunity. He kicked the wire mesh away and dropped down into the room.

For the second time today Jake had a chance, however slim, to save the world, and he wasn't going to waste it. He took a deep breath and approached the main computer.

That's when he heard a sound that made his blood run cold. It was a toilet flushing. There was someone else there! Before Jake was able to hide, another technician walked in through the toilet door on the other side of the room. Jake silently cursed his luck as the technician stared at him in disbelief.

In an instant, the technician stood in front of the door, drew a gun and pointed it straight at Jake.

"Don't move a muscle."

Using his radio, the technician called Jean-Paul. Jake didn't know what was going to happen when he arrived; all he knew for sure was that he was sick of this place. Moments later, the door slid open and Jean-Paul walked in. He stood in front of Jake smiling broadly with his arms folded.

"You just won't behave, will you?" he said, ruffling Jake's hair patronisingly. Jake batted his hand away but Jean-Paul simply smiled.

"Out of interest," he continued, "what was your plan? I took your little DVD."

"I was going to break the hypnosis myself!" said Jake, glaring at Jean-Paul.

Jean-Paul's smile widened and he began chuckling to himself. Before long, the laugh had grown into a full-blown roar. As he watched Jean-Paul laughing, Jake was suddenly filled with a hatred that he had never felt for anyone in his life. How dare this evil maniac laugh at him!

"I've got to admit, I'm a little disappointed," Jean-Paul said between laughs. "I expected more of you than that!" Jake clenched his fists involuntarily as he continued, "I mean, didn't you do your research? You should know that my programme is unbreakable. Just face it, you kids can't stand in the way of progress."

"Prove it!" said Jake.

"What?" replied Jean-Paul.

"Prove it," said Jake again. "If the hypnosis is as unbreakable as you say, then you won't mind me having a go. Think of it as a challenge."

Jean-Paul thought for a moment, then smiled. "I like you," he said. "You don't give up. Fair enough," said Jean-Paul. "Be my guest!"

"Sir!" said the technician, shocked that Jean-Paul

was letting this happen.

"Relax," said Jean-Paul. "The programme is perfect! He doesn't stand a chance."

"But, Sir –"

"Set up the global broadcast system – now," said Jean-Paul to the technician, with a threatening tone in his voice.

The technician approached the computer uneasily. He tapped a few buttons, then glanced nervously back at Jean-Paul. "It's ready," he said, still not happy about the idea.

"Go ahead," said Jean-Paul, smirking. "Speak into the camera and the computer will translate it into all the languages of the world. You'll be speaking to around six billion people. No pressure though..."

Jake approached the computer and looked up at the camera. It was now or never. He took a deep breath and started to speak.

"This is a message for everyone who..." Jake paused; how do you put something like this into words? "For everyone who..." Jake paused again, and panicked as he realised that he had no idea what to say. He heard Jean-Paul laughing behind him and he felt the rush of anger returning. He had to wipe that smile off Jean-Paul's face!

"Remember when you could go outside and ride a bike, or play football?" Jake began nervously. "Remember when you could smile and laugh?" he continued. "You can't do any of those things any more. Powerball is the reason for that. Your addiction to this game has stolen your mind, your freedom – and your life!" said Jake, with tears welling up in his eyes. "Powerball is comfortable and safe, I know! But it's not real. Life is real! Yeah, it can be hard at times, but it can also be amazing and beautiful. Powerball is just nothingness, endless nothingness..."

Jake began to get nervous. He could sense that it wasn't working. He thought about his mum and how much he loved and missed her, how much he wished that she would just wake up. Hang on, he thought. He certainly wasn't the only one who felt that way about another person. Maybe that was the key! Love for other people – that was the only way that he could remind the world of how good it was to be alive.

He decided to make one last, desperate plea. "Please, think about your loved ones: your wives, husbands, children, mothers, fathers," continued Jake, and his voice became a croak as he pictured his own mum, sitting motionless on the couch. He ignored the sniggering from Jean-Paul behind him and continued. "I know you miss them, underneath the layers of numbness that Powerball has driven into your mind. They're what's important. Please, remember the people you love and fight for them. It's not too late to get them back! Just unplug the machine and go outside! Take your life back!"

"That's enough," said Jean-Paul.

"Take your life back!" shouted Jake into the camera again before Jean-Paul turned it off.

"Thank you," said Jean-Paul. "You've been very entertaining. But now I think I should get you back to your friends. You have to finish your training."

"Umm, Sir…" said the technician.

"What is it?" snapped Jean-Paul.

"Something strange is happening," he began, staring at a computer screen. "People are switching off their machines."

"What?" shouted Jean-Paul.

"How many?"

"About four per cent of the population," he said.

"Four per cent?" said Jean-Paul, "A measly two hundred million people," he said dismissively. "That's just a technical glitch! Happens all the time."

"Hang on," said the technician. "It's rising!"

"To what?" said Jean-Paul, starting to sound vaguely concerned.

"Twenty per cent, no wait! Forty! Sixty!"

"Nooooo!" yelled Jean-Paul, turning to face Jake – but Jake wasn't there. He had taken the brief opportunity to run, which was just as well because if Jean-Paul had caught him at this moment he'd probably have killed him.

"One hundred per cent of the population!" said the technician, incredulously.

It was true. Across the world, people who had been inside for weeks were emerging into the sunlight. They greeted friends, family and neighbours that they hadn't seen in ages and breathed in the fresh air. Of course, they had no idea what was going on, but they enjoyed the feeling of freedom.

Jean-Paul, on the other hand, was not enjoying himself one bit. He clenched his fists and screamed as he saw his dream crumbling before his eyes.

"It's all over," he shouted, enraged. "Engage 'plan X' immediately!"

"Are you sure?" said the technician.

"Do it!" bellowed Jean-Paul.

pride comes before a fall
part two

Jake was rushing through the building when he heard the piercing screech of the warning buzzer. "Warning! Self-destruct sequence initiated. Detonation in five minutes," proclaimed a loud, computerised voice.

Jake froze in his tracks as he tried to figure out what was happening. Jean-Paul must know he's beaten, thought Jake. He must be trying to cover his tracks, trying to destroy all the evidence!

Jake shook himself as he realised that the reasons behind Jean-Paul blowing up the building weren't important right now. He had only five minutes to save Robert and Sarah from being blown to bits! He raced along the corridors, but soon he was lost. The rooms all looked the same and the fact that everyone in the building was running for his or her life didn't exactly help Jake concentrate.

After two minutes of precious time wasted on running aimlessly around the building, Jake found the screening room where Sarah and Robert were being held. As people pushed past him on all sides, he looked through the small window in the door. He could see Robert and Sarah inside. He'd never been this happy to see two people in his whole life.

Obviously, Robert and Sarah were pretty pleased to see him, too.

"It's Jake," shouted Sarah. "We're saved!"

"Don't speak too soon," warned Robert, as the pair watched Jake's attempts to batter down the door with his shoulder.

Jake was a strong boy but the door to the screening room was reinforced. It would have taken a battering ram to get through it.

Robert and Sarah watched Jake looking through the window at them. He seemed to be panicking – he had no idea how to get to them.

Sarah took a deep breath and approached the window. "Just go, Jake," she said.

"What?" said Robert.

"He can't save us, Robert," said Sarah, "but he can still save himself."

"No!" cried Jake through the glass.

"Go! Go now!" shouted Sarah.

Jake took a final look at Sarah and Robert and then disappeared.

"I can't believe he left us!" said Robert, throwing his hands into the air. "We're goners!"

"He had no choice," said Sarah to herself.

"Detonation in two minutes," intoned the electronic voice.

What Robert didn't realise was that, rather than running out of the building, which might have been the sensible thing to do at this point, Jake was running up to the roof. He hadn't given up on saving them.

Jake sprinted up stairs to the roof, taking the steps three at a time, with his lungs burning and his heart pounding. When he got to a door that said 'Rooftop Access' he charged through it, just hearing the computerised voice say "Detonation in thirty seconds," as he stepped out into the daylight.

He ran to the hoverpod and jumped into the driver's seat. He hammered the ignition and flew the hoverpod round in a wide arcing loop to the east side of the building. He pointed the nose of the machine to the window of what he thought was the screening room and closed his eyes tight.

Sarah and Robert saw him coming just in time to dive out of the way as the flying machine crashed through the window.

"Get in!" Jake screamed.

Sarah and Robert dived into the now battered hoverpod as Jake was taking off again. He quickly turned the hoverpod around and accelerated back out of the hole that he had just made in the window. Seconds later, they heard the most enormous explosion from behind them.

Sarah looked behind her and saw the blast tear the building apart. Concrete and steel, that had been sturdy and permanent only seconds before, was now twisting and shattering before her eyes. She looked at Jake. If it wasn't for him they would still be in there.

"Thank you," she said.

"Don't mention it," replied Jake.

The next few days were very confusing. People all over the world had woken up with no idea what had been going on for the last few weeks. The one thing they did know was that they didn't want to play Powerball any more; they didn't even want a Razon 500. Dustbins around the world were filled with the consoles and, soon enough, people had forgotten the craze, blissfully ignorant of how close they'd come to global war.

There were, to tell the whole truth, a few people who weren't ignorant of the goings-on at Razon HQ.

A couple of days after the explosion, Mrs Emily Austen, the director of the Secret Intelligence Service MI6, received a very interesting package. It contained a long letter explaining exactly what had happened over the last weeks. It described how Jean-Paul had used Powerball to enslave the world and how close he had come to starting World War III. She immediately launched an investigation.

The more she checked into the story, the more everything in the letter seemed to make sense. A couple of months later, using information from the letter, MI6 caught Jean-Paul. When they questioned him, all he would talk about was the mysterious group of kids that had foiled his plans: the same kids, Emily assumed, who had written the letter.

It was clear that there was a new crime-fighting force on the scene – one that was young, brave and ready for anything.

Around the corridors of MI6 they soon became known simply as 'The M.I.Five'.

grown-ups are good for something

part one

Alex and Chun Mai sat in the computer room watching the security camera footage from the Razon building. They stared in horror as their friends fell slowly under Jean-Paul's spell. Soon Chun Mai couldn't watch any more. She flicked off the screen and held her head in her hands.

"We failed," she said, her voice cracking as tears welled up in her eyes. Alex looked at her with pity. He wanted desperately to say something to make it better but there was nothing he could think of. She was right, there was no more they could do. The plan had failed, the world was doomed to eternal slavery.

The pair sat in silence for a long time until Alex finally spoke.

"Well," he said, "maybe we can't save the world – but we can save Robert, Sarah and Jake!" Chun Mai looked at him, unsure what he meant. "Come on," he added, standing up purposefully.

Robert led Chun Mai across the grounds to the barn. He pushed open the door and revealed the second hoverpod. When Chun Mai had last seen this machine it had been in a very bad way indeed, but now it seemed almost as good as new.

"You fixed it!" she said. "How? When?"

"I couldn't sleep last night," he said, "so I thought I might as well make myself useful."

"Good job you did," said Chun Mai, not for the first time baffled and impressed by the technological brilliance of her friend. She jumped into the passenger seat. "Let's go," she said impatiently.

Alex jumped in after her and pressed the ignition button. "Come on, old girl," he said as the engine stuttered and clanked. The machine lurched into the air and he carefully piloted the hoverpod out of the barn. He climbed to about a hundred metres and fired the boosters. There was a loud bang as they set off, and when Chun Mai looked behind her she saw thick puffs of black smoke coming out of the engine.

"Is that normal?" she asked.

"Oh yeah, of course," said Alex.

"You're a terrible liar," replied Chun Mai.

There wasn't a great deal of conversation on the way to Poland. Both Alex and Chun Mai were hugely depressed about the mission. They were both used to succeeding at everything they did and neither of them much liked this new feeling of failure. However, as they got closer to Poland, they focused their minds on the task in hand. There was no way that they were going to let Jean-Paul enslave their friends.

As they approached the building, Alex engaged the cloaking device and was able to fly right up to the window of the room where the rest of the team were being held.

"There they are," said Chun Mai when she spotted them. "Okay, wish me luck," she said, as she unbuckled her safety belt and slung her laptop bag over her shoulder.

"Good luck," whispered Alex, wincing as he watched his friend open the hoverpod's side hatch and clamber out on to the bonnet.

Chun Mai wasn't a tremendous fan of heights and right now she liked them even less than normal. She had made the mistake of looking down to the ground below and suddenly felt extremely nauseous. She clung on to the bonnet of the hoverpod for dear life as the wind buffeted her from side to side. "Come on, Chun Mai, now or never," she said out loud to herself, as she eyed the narrow ledge in front of the screening room window. It was only a metre away, she could easily jump it, couldn't she? She imagined herself on dry land hopping over a puddle and tried to fool herself into thinking that this was no different. She took a deep breath and jumped.

Alex gasped as he saw Chun Mai wobble, her feet struggling for grip on the ledge, but she soon stabilised herself, breathing heavy sighs of relief as she leant against the glass. She gave Alex a thumbs up and he piloted the hoverpod upwards into the sky.

As Chun Mai watched her friends transfixed by Powerball, she fished in her pocket for a small crystal glass-cutter, one of Alex's tools. Still teetering on the brink of the ledge, she began to cut a large circle in the window. When it was big enough for her to fit through, she tapped it lightly and a perfect circle of glass shattered on to the floor of the screening room. She picked up her walkie-talkie and spoke to Alex.

"Okay, Alex, do it," she said.

Alex had flown the hoverpod up to the roof and was now standing in front of the main electrical fuse box with a pair of heavy bolt cutters. When Chun Mai gave the word, he cut through a carefully chosen wire and every electrical appliance in the entire east side of the Razon building suddenly turned off.

When Chun Mai saw the Powerball demo flicker off, along with every light in the room, she knew that it was safe to enter. She carefully ducked through the hole in the glass, ran to the front of the room and opened her laptop. She slid a copy of the antidote DVD into the laptop's disk drive and sat back.

It worked like a charm. Within a couple of minutes

the expression was returning to the faces of her friends, and soon after that, they began to speak.

"Chun Mai?" gasped Sarah, bewildered. "What are you doing here?"

"I'm saving you," she said with a wink.

Just then, Chun Mai jumped with fright as she noticed Jean-Paul's face at the window in the door. "Hey!" he said. "What's going on in there?"

"That's all I need," said Chun Mai, quickly ushering the others towards the window. "Get here now, Alex!" she shouted into her walkie-talkie.

"Open this door immediately!" shouted Jean-Paul from outside.

"The door lock's electronic," said Chun Mai. "We've cut the power, he can't get in." They heard a huge bang from just outside the door. Jean-Paul was shooting at the lock in an attempt to get in. "Unless he does that, of course," added Chun Mai, flustered.

The kids quickly filtered out on to the ledge, one by one, until they were all lined up with their backs to the glass, trying not to look at the sheer drop below.

"Please tell me this isn't the extent of your plan," said Robert.

"Come on, Alex! Now!" yelled Chun Mai into the walkie-talkie.

Two more gunshots echoed behind them. Having shot through the lock, Jean-Paul kicked it open with little difficulty.

"Stop right there!" he shouted, pointing his gun straight at them. The kids did as they were told. "I didn't realise there were more of you lot," he said. "You kids are becoming more trouble than you're worth, you know!"

Chun Mai glanced down and saw Alex in the hoverpod just below them. She subtly gestured to the others. "Jump on three!" she said, quietly.

"Come back in here now and I might just spare some of you," said Jean-Paul, smirking.

"Three!" shouted Chun Mai in a panic, and they all jumped on to the roof of the hoverpod.

As they scrabbled around for something to hold on to, Jake found himself sliding down the bonnet of the hoverpod. As he neared the edge, and the fatal drop that came after it, he felt a firm hand on the collar of his shirt. "Careful, mate," said Robert, as he hauled Jake back on to the roof.

Jean-Paul couldn't believe his eyes. They had jumped out of a fourth floor window! He rushed over and leant out, expecting to see splattered children, but was instead clouted around the head by the back end of the hoverpod as it rose up past the window.

"Let's get out of here!" cried Sarah, as Alex fired the boosters and raced away from the building. The kids clung to the roof until Alex found a safe place to set down so that they could all squeeze inside.

When they got back to the manor house, the kids had mixed feelings. Of course they were happy not to be hypnotised, and to be alive for that matter, but still, they were painfully aware that they hadn't actually achieved anything. The world was still hypnotised by Jean-Paul, and they were back to square one.

The kids were lying around in the lounge reflecting on this when a thought suddenly occurred to Jake. Well, not a thought exactly, more a vague memory –

the after effects of the hypnosis had left him with a fuzzy memory of the last twelve hours. Whatever it was, his gut feeling told him he needed to go and check something, so he stood up and left the room.

Moments later he came charging back into the lounge, bursting with excitement and brandishing a mobile phone.

"Guys, guys!" he said, excitedly.

"What is it, Jake?" asked Robert.

"I've just remembered something," Jake blurted out, almost too excited to speak. "When Jean-Paul's guards captured me they forgot to take my phone!"

"So?" said Alex.

"I used the voice record function to record him speaking. I've got the whole thing on tape." The kids looked back at him blankly. "Don't you see? This is proof of what Jean-Paul's planning!"

"It might be proof, Jake, but who's going to listen to us?" said Robert.

"Yeah, Jake, we tried that," said Chun Mai. "They aren't interested."

"That was *then*!" said Jake. "They can't possibly deny that something's going on now – and we can prove exactly what's happening!"

"He's got a point," said Sarah. "The rules are different now! We can go straight to the Prime Minister! If we break his hypnosis and explain, he just might believe us..."

"It's a long shot..." said Robert.

"But it's the only shot we've got," replied Sarah.

"Okay," said Chun Mai. "Let's do it!"

"Great, we'll take the car!" said Sarah pacing out of the room, closely followed by Jake.

"What car?" chorused Robert, Chun Mai and Alex.

grown-ups are good for something part two

The drive from Cumbria to London normally takes the best part of six hours, but with Sarah driving a fast sports car along roads with no traffic, it took half that. Only Jake, who had experienced Sarah's driving before, didn't feel the need to cling on to the armrests out of sheer panic.

Finally, they arrived at Downing Street and gazed down at the famous number 10, home to the Prime Minister. They rested their arms on the large black gates that protect the street and contemplated the strangeness of the situation.

"Let's go," said Sarah as she began to climb the gates. The others followed her example and soon all five were clambering over the top. Under normal circumstances, armed guards would appear and arrest you immediately if you tried to break in – but these were far from normal circumstances.

"How're we going to get in?" asked Jake when they arrived outside the famous black front door.

"It is a little known fact that the front door of 10 Downing Street is never locked," said Sarah, pushing the heavy door open.

"Why?" said Jake, astonished.

"Because there's always an armed guard inside and outside," she said, before glancing up and down the completely empty street and adding, "Normally."

The kids filed into the building. The fact that this had already been a fairly unusual day did nothing to diminish the strangeness of being in the Prime Minister's private home and office. The only person who seemed comfortable in the pristine formal hallways was Sarah – she was a big fan of politics and, although she would never admit it, secretly hoped to be Prime Minister herself one day.

She had read several books about the building, so she knew precisely where she was going. She led the kids to a small staircase and couldn't resist showing off a little more of her knowledge.

"This is the stairway to the Prime Minister's private quarters," she said. "It's lined with portraits and photographs of all the British Prime Ministers there have ever been."

They began to ascend the stairs. As they walked past picture after picture of history's great Prime Ministers, the importance of what they were about to do began to dawn on them. Jake started to worry: what if the Prime Minister didn't believe them? After all, even he hadn't believed it at first.

Sarah led them through the Prime Minister's private apartment to the small mahogany door that led to his study. They could hear the noises of Powerball loud and clear through the door.

"Right guys," she said. "When we get in there don't look at the screen. Chun Mai, you switch the disks.

Robert and Jake, you grab the Prime Minister so that he can't stop her."

Grab the Prime Minister? thought Jake. That's not the kind of instruction you get every day.

Sarah pushed open the door and the kids rushed in. Jake and Robert caught hold of the Prime Minister while Chun Mai ejected the Powerball disk.

"Get your hands off me!" shouted the Prime Minister in a rage.

"Very sorry, Sir," said Jake.

"You'll thank us later," added Robert, "I hope..."

Chun Mai slid in the antidote game DVD and the Prime Minister gradually stopped fighting and began to watch. A few minutes later he was blinking and looking around the room. He was back to his former self, although, understandably, very confused.

"Who are you?" he said. "How did you get in?"

"Let me explain, Sir," said Sarah.

A day later, Jean-Paul had almost forgotten the kids. He had a lump on his head caused by the collision with the hoverpod, but beyond that he wasn't too worried about them. After all, what could five kids do against the man in charge of the whole world?

He was in his private office, reviewing the final plans for his great war, when he heard a hammering on the door. He opened it to find one of his guards with a grim expression on his face.

"Sir," said the guard, "we're under attack!"

"What do you mean?" said Jean-Paul.

"The army, Sir! They're coming!" replied the guard.

Jean-Paul laughed. Surely this must be some kind of bad joke. The expression on the guard's face remained deadly serious and Jean-Paul's laughter faded. He hurried over to his window and looked down. Sure enough, a fleet of tanks was approaching fast.

"How is this possible?" yelled Jean-Paul.

"What shall we do, Sir?" asked the guard, but Jean-Paul didn't have an answer. He simply pushed past him and ran into the hallway.

How had the army found out? He thought, as he raced up a flight of stairs to the roof. He intended to make an escape in his helicopter, but when he opened the door he was confronted by the twenty Royal Marines who had just arrived by parachute.

"Put your hands up, Mr Laurent. Let's not have any fuss," said one of them.

Faced with the sight of twenty highly trained men pointing guns at him, Jean-Paul did the sensible thing and surrendered immediately.

Back at 10 Downing Street, the kids were enjoying tea and cakes with the Prime Minister and a few of his senior advisors. Once the Prime Minister had recovered from the initial shock of being woken, it hadn't taken long to explain the situation to him. He was a very intelligent man who was willing to listen, even to children. The more the kids told him and showed him, the more things began to make sense.

Once the Prime Minister was on board, they spent the day waking people up. Naturally they started with the Prime Minister's key staff. When they had all decided upon a plan, Jake, Robert, Chun Mai and Alex were dispatched to military bases across the country to wake the soldiers and pilots that would be required to go out to Poland to bring Jean-Paul to justice.

Sarah stayed behind to continue filling the Prime Minister in on what had happened while he'd been asleep, a task that she was honoured to carry out.

Now, with the whole team reunited in London, they waited for news of the mission. Eventually, a man in a military general's uniform entered the room. "The mission was a complete success!" he said. "We have Jean-Paul Laurent and his entire organisation in custody, and the antidote DVD is playing from Razon HQ as we speak," he added with a smile.

"Thank you and very well done, General Roberts," said the Prime Minister.

The kids hugged each other ecstatically, whooping and cheering boisterously. The Prime Minister smiled; this sort of behaviour wasn't expected in the cabinet room but he was prepared to make an exception. He looked around the table at the kids who had literally saved the world, shook his head and laughed a little. He still couldn't really believe what had happened.

Making powerful and persuasive speeches is a big

part of a politician's job, but at this moment even the Prime Minister couldn't think of a way to put the sheer size of the kids' achievement into words.

The Prime Minister smiled and stood up. He raised his teacup and toasted his new friends. "To the Mega Intelligent Five!" he said.

"To us!" they responded proudly, raising their cups in the air.

It was decided that the general population didn't need to know how close they had come to being involved in the biggest war that the world had ever seen. Ordinary people were told that a hypnotic element had been included in the game by accident. Happy with this explanation, they soon returned to their jobs, friends and normal lives.

As a result of this cover-up the kids did not receive the recognition they deserved – but they didn't mind. The safety of the world was all the reward they needed. However, the people who did know the truth were left in no doubt about the kids' abilities. It was clear that there was a new crime-fighting force on the scene: one that was young, brave and ready for anything.

That force was suitably named 'The M.I.Five'.

WARNING!

The following dossier is highly classified

MI6 Internal Memo:
*Preliminary information on the group
of mega-intelligent children, code
named the M.I.Five*

Name: Jake Robinson
Nationality: British
Assumed Age: 12
Hair Colour: Brown
Eyes: Green
Status: At large

Notes:
**Though little is known about Jake prior to the last few
weeks, surveillance reports indicate that his particular
speciality is maths. According to his former teachers, Jake's
exam scores were off the charts, particularly when it came
to problem-solving and mathematical codes.**

**In addition to this skill, Jake is highly capable when it
comes to dangerous missions, and is thought to be one of
the bravest members of the team.**
**Even though it appears that Jake only joined the
organisation recently, he seems to be fitting in perfectly.**

Name: Sarah Ellen Moore

Nationality: British

Assumed Age: 11–12

Hair Colour: Red/brown

Eyes: Green

Status: At large

CONFIDENTIAL

Notes:

It is believed that Sarah is the daughter of Duncan Moore, the British ambassador to France. As such, she has developed a healthy interest in world affairs and a phenomenal gift for languages. Our agents indicate that she currently speaks at least five foreign languages fluently.

Of the entire group, Sarah in particular exhibits judgement, bravery and resourcefulness far beyond her years. She appears to be the closest thing the M.I.Five have to a leader, though this is not thought to be an official title.

Name: Alex Brady

Nationality: British

CONFIDENTIAL

Assumed Age: 12

Hair Colour: Black

Eyes: Brown

Status: At large

Notes:

Considering this boy's intelligence and extreme talent for invention, it's amazing that we haven't heard about him until now, particularly since he often draws attention to himself by causing large explosions.

Surveillance photographs of the technology developed by Brady have even our top MI6 scientists baffled. It is clear to all that he possesses a scientific talent that easily equals that of great minds like Newton or Einstein. He must be watched very carefully.

There are also some unproven reports that Brady has developed a highly sophisticated flying machine, though for some reason our agents have been unable to produce a photograph of it.

CONFIDENTIAL

Name: Robert Hastings, a.k.a 'The Great Roberto'
Nationality: British
Assumed Age: 12
Hair Colour: Blonde
Eyes: Blue
Status: At large

Notes:
Information on Robert Hastings has not been hard to come by, as he's something of a celebrity.

In his life as popular child magician 'The Great Roberto', Robert has received the adulation of thousands of fans in countries around the world. It would appear that this acclaim has gone to his head, as he often displays an extremely confident air that borders on cockiness.

However, he is a highly intelligent boy and an incredibly skilled magician. It is believed that his magic skills often come in handy during missions.

In addition to being a famous magician, Robert is the son of a wealthy aristocratic family who own the manor house that the M.I.Five are currently using as a base. It is thought that Robert's parents are unaware of this arrangement.

Name: Chun Mai

CONFIDENTIAL

Nationality: South Korean

Assumed Age: 10 (Possibly younger)

Hair Colour: Black

Eyes: Brown

Status: At large

Notes:

Unbelievable as it may sound, given her tender age, Chun Mai appears to be one of the most advanced computer hackers in the world. From the little information we have been able to gather about her skills, it seems that Chun Mai's abilities are practically unparalleled, even amongst those twice her age.

So incredible are her skills that many believe we may have finally found the true identity of 'The Jester', the legendary hacker who somehow managed to gain access to both the MI6 and CIA computer networks last year. No hard evidence for this has surfaced yet, though MI6 security would very much like a chance to speak to her.